She lifted an eyebrow and hid the delighted smile she felt inside. "Clear to where, Connor?"

He straightened up. "Doesn't matter." He inhaled sharply. "What does matter is that every guy in here is looking, too."

Okay, there was just a tiny stirring of uneasiness. She'd *wanted* Connor to get an eyeful, and she'd known she might attract some attention from other guys. But the thought of a room full of marines checking her out gave her a chill that wasn't quite the thrill she might have guessed. But she wasn't going to let Connor know it! "And how is this any of your business?" she asked.

"We're friends, Em," he said. "I'm just trying to look out for you. That's all."

She didn't believe him for a minute. There was a flash of something dark and dangerous in his eyes and it didn't have a thing to do with feelings for his *pal.* Okay, fine, She'd play along. The longer he tried to hold out against her, the harder she'd make it for him. Because she was determined to be the cause for his losing the bet, after all....

Dear Reader,

Thank you for choosing Silhouette Desire, where this month we have six fabulous novels for you to enjoy. We start things off with *Estate Affair* by Sara Orwig, the latest installment of the continuing DYNASTIES: THE ASHTONS series. In this upstairs/downstairs-themed story, the Ashtons' maid falls for an Ashton son and all sorts of scandal follows. And in Maureen Child's *Whatever Reilly Wants...*, the second title in the THREE-WAY WAGER series, a sexy marine gets an unexpected surprise when he falls for his suddenly transformed gal pal.

Susan Crosby concludes her BEHIND CLOSED DOORS series with *Secrets of Paternity*. The secret baby in this book just happens to be eighteen years old.... Hmm, there's quite the story behind that revelation. The wonderful Emilie Rose presents *Scandalous Passion*, a sultry tale of a woman desperate to get back some steamy photos from her past lover. Of course, he has a price for returning those pictures, but it's not money he's after. *The Sultan's Bed*, by Laura Wright, continues the tales of her sheikh heroes with an enigmatic male who is searching for his missing sister and finds a startling attraction to her lovely neighbor. And finally, what was supposed to be just an elevator ride turns into a very passionate encounter, in *Blame It on the Blackout* by Heidi Betts.

Sit back and enjoy all of the smart, sensual stories Silhouette Desire has to offer.

Happy reading,

*Melissa Jeglinski*

Melissa Jeglinski
Senior Editor
Silhouette Desire

Please address questions and book requests to:
Silhouette Reader Service
U.S.: 3010 Walden Ave., P.O. Box 1325, Buffalo, NY 14269
Canadian: P.O. Box 609, Fort Erie, Ont. L2A 5X3

# Whatever REILLY Wants...

## MAUREEN CHILD

Silhouette® Desire

Published by Silhouette Books

**America's Publisher of Contemporary Romance**

SILHOUETTE BOOKS

ISBN 0-373-76658-0

WHATEVER REILLY WANTS…

Copyright © 2005 by Maureen Child

This edition published by arrangement with Harlequin Books S.A.

Visit Silhouette Books at www.eHarlequin.com

**Printed in U.S.A.**

## MAUREEN CHILD

is a California native who loves to travel. Every chance they get, she and her husband are taking off on another research trip. The author of more than sixty books, Maureen loves a happy ending and still swears that she has the best job in the world. She lives in Southern California with her husband, two children and a golden retriever with delusions of grandeur.

Visit her Web site at www.maureenchild.com.

For Kathleen Beaver.
Thanks for being an emergency reader,
for always being a friend
and for never getting tired of meeting me
for a latte to talk about writing!

# One

"**O**ne down, two to go." Father Liam Reilly grinned at his brother, sitting alongside him, then lifted a beer in salute to the two identical men sitting opposite him in the restaurant booth.

"Don't get your hopes up." Connor Reilly took a sip of his own beer and nodded toward his brother Brian, the third of the Reilly triplets, sitting beside Liam. "Just because Brian couldn't go the distance, doesn't mean we can't."

"Amen," Aidan said from beside him.

"Who said I *couldn't* go the distance?" Brian demanded, reaching for a handful of tortilla chips from the basket in the middle of the table. He grinned and sat back in the booth. "I just didn't *want* to go the distance. Not anymore." He held up his left hand, and the gold wedding band caught the light and winked at all of them.

"And I'm glad for you," Liam said, his black eyebrows lifting. "Plus, with you happily married, the odds of *my* winning this bet are better than ever."

"Not a chance, Liam." Aidan grabbed a handful of chips, too. "It's not that I begrudge you a roof for the church...but *I'm* the Reilly to watch in this bet, brother."

As his brothers talked, Connor just smiled and half listened. Once a week the Reilly brothers met for dinner at the Lighthouse Restaurant, a family place, dead center of the town of Baywater. They laughed, talked and, in general, enjoyed the camaraderie of being brothers.

But for the last month their conversations had pretty much centered around *The Bet.*

A great uncle, the last surviving member of a set of triplets, had left ten thousand dollars to Aidan, Brian and Connor. At first, the three of them had thought to divide the money, giving their older brother, Liam, an equal share. Then someone, and Connor was pretty sure it had been Liam, had come up with the idea of a bet—winner take all.

Since the Reilly triplets were, above all things, competitive, there'd never been any real doubt that they would accept the challenge. But Liam hadn't made it easy. He'd insisted that as a Catholic priest, his decision to give up sex for a lifetime was something not one of his brothers could match. He dared them to be celibate for ninety days—last man standing winning the ten thousand dollars. And if all three of the triplets failed, then Liam got the money for a new roof for his church.

Connor shot his older brother a suspicious look. He had a feeling that Liam was already getting estimates from local roofers. Scowling, he took another sip of his beer and let his gaze shift to Brian. A month ago the triplets had stood together in this bet, but now one had already fallen. Brian had reconciled with his ex-wife, Tina, and, now there was just Connor and Aidan to survive the bet.

"Don't know about you," Aidan said, jamming his elbow into Connor's rib cage, "but I'm avoiding all females for the duration."

"No self-control, huh?" Liam grinned and lifted his beer for another long drink.

"You're really enjoying this, aren't you?" Connor glared at him.

"Damn right I am," Liam said laughing. "Watching the three of you has always been entertaining. Just more so lately."

"Ah," Brian said, "the *two* of them. I'm out, remember?"

"Didn't even last a month," Aidan said with a slow, sad shake of his head.

Brian's self-satisfied smile spoke volumes. "Never been so glad about losing a bet in my life."

"Tina's a peach, no doubt about it," Connor said,

just a little irritated by Brian's "happy man" attitude. "But there's still the matter of you in that ridiculous outfit to consider."

Not only did the losers lose the money in this bet, but they'd agreed to ride around in the back of a convertible, wearing coconut bras and hula skirts while being driven around the base on Battle Color day…the one day of the year when every dignitary imaginable would be on the Marine base.

Brian shuddered, then manfully sucked it up and squared his shoulders. "It'll still be worth it."

"He's got it bad," Aidan muttered, and held up both index fingers in an impromptu cross, as if trying to keep Brian at a distance.

"Laugh all you want," Brian said, leaning over the table to stare first at one brother, then the other. "But I'm the only one here having regular—and can I just add—*great,* sex."

"That was cold, man." Aidan groaned and scraped one hand over his face.

"Heartless," Connor agreed.

Liam laughed, clapped his hands together, then rubbed his palms briskly. Black eyebrows lifting, he looked at his brothers and asked, "Either of you care to back out now? Save time?"

"Not likely," Aidan muttered.

"That's for damn sure." Connor held out one hand to Aidan. "In this to the end?"

Aidan's grip was fierce. "Or until you cave. Whichever comes first."

"In your dreams." Connor'd never lost a bet yet and he wasn't about to start with this one. Of course, the stakes were higher and the bet more challenging than anything else he'd ever done, but that didn't matter. This was about *pride*. And he'd be damned if he'd let Aidan beat him. Besides, "No way am I gonna be riding in that convertible with Brian."

"I'll save you a seat," Brian said, grinning.

"Oh, man, I need another beer." Aidan lifted one hand to get the waitress's attention.

Another beer would be good. All he had to do was *not* look at the waitress. Connor's gaze snapped from Aidan to Brian and finally to Liam. "This game's far from over, you know."

"There's two, count 'em, *two* long, tempting months left," Liam reminded him.

"Yeah, well, don't be picking out roof shingles just yet, *Father.*"

Liam just smiled. "The samples are coming tomorrow."

The next morning Connor sat in the sunlight outside Jake's Garage and sighed heavily. South Carolina in July. Even the mornings were hot and steamy. The heat flattened a man until all he wanted to do was either escape to a beach and ocean breezes or find a nice shady tree and park himself beneath it.

Neither of which Connor was doing. He was on leave. Two weeks off and nothing to do. Hell, he didn't even want to go anywhere. What would be the point? He couldn't date. Couldn't spend any time at all with a woman the way he was feeling. He was a man on the edge.

Two more months of this bet and he wasn't sure how he was going to survive. Connor *liked* women. He liked the way they smelled and the way they laughed and the way they moved. He liked dancing with 'em, walking with 'em and most especially, he liked making love to 'em.

So he'd never found the *one*.

Who said he was looking for her?

His mother, Maggie, had been telling her sons the story of her own whirlwind courtship and marriage to their father since they were kids. They'd all heard about the lightning bolt that had hit Maggie and Sean Reilly. About how they'd shared a dance at a town picnic, fallen desperately in love and within two weeks had been married. Nine months later, Liam had arrived and just two years later, the triplets.

Maggie had long been a big believer in love at first sight and had always insisted that when the time was right, each of her sons…well, except for Liam, would be hit by a thunderbolt.

Connor had made it a point to steer clear of storms.

"Boy, you look like you could chew glass." Emma Jacobsen, owner and manager of Jake's Garage, took a seat on the bench beside him.

Connor smiled. Here was the one woman he could trust himself with. The one woman he'd never thought of as, well…a *woman*.

She wore dark-blue coveralls and a white T-shirt beneath. Her long, blond hair was pulled back into a ponytail and braided, falling to the middle of her back. She had a smudge of grease across her nose, and the cap she wore shaded her blue eyes. She'd been his friend for two years, and he could honestly say he'd never once wondered what she looked like under those coveralls.

Emma was safety.

"It's this damn bet," Connor muttered, and leaned his elbows on the bench back behind him, stretching out his legs and crossing them at the ankles.

"So why'd you agree to it in the first place?"

He grinned. "Turn down a challenge?"

She laughed. "What was I thinking?"

"Exactly." He shook his head and sighed. "But it's harder than I thought it'd be. I'm telling you, Em, I spend most of my time avoiding women like the plague. Hell, I even crossed the street yesterday when I saw a gorgeous redhead coming my way."

"Poor baby."

"Sarcasm isn't pretty."

"Yeah, but so appropriate." She smiled and punched his shoulder. "So if you're avoiding women, what're you doing hanging around *my* place?"

Straightening up, Connor dropped one arm around her shoulder and gave her a quick, comradely squeeze. "That's the beauty of it, Em. I'm *safe* here."

"Huh?"

He looked at the confusion on her face and explained. "I can hang out with you and not worry. I've never *wanted* you. Not that way. So being here is like finding a demilitarized zone in the middle of a war."

"You've never wanted me."

"We're pals, Em." Connor gave her another squeeze just to prove how much he thought of her. "We can talk cars. You don't expect me to bring you flowers or open doors for you. You're not a *woman*, you're a *mechanic*."

Emma Virginia Jacobsen stared at the man sitting next to her and wondered why she wasn't shrieking. He'd never *wanted* her? She wasn't a *woman?*

For two years Connor Reilly had been coming to the shop she'd inherited from her father when he passed away five years ago. For two years she'd known Connor and listened to him talk about whatever female he might be chasing at the moment. She'd laughed with him, joked with him and had always thought he was different. She'd believed that he'd looked *beyond* her being female—that he'd seen her as a woman *and* as a friend.

*Now* she finds out he didn't even think of her as female *at all?*

Fury erupted inside her while she futilely tried to reign it in. Not once in the past two years had she even considered going after Connor Reilly herself. Not that he wasn't attractive or anything. While he continued to talk, she glanced at his profile.

His black hair was cut militarily short. His features were clean and sharp. High cheekbones, square jaw, clear, dark-blue eyes that sparkled when he laughed. He wore a dark-green USMC T-shirt that strained across his muscular chest and a pair of dark-green running shorts that showed off long, tanned, very hairy legs.

Okay, sure, he was gorgeous, but Emma had never thought of him as dating material because of their friendship. Now, she was glad she *hadn't* gone after him. He would have laughed in her face.

And that thought only tossed gasoline on the fires of anger burning inside her.

"So you can see," he was saying, "why it's so nice to have this place to hang out. If I want to win this bet—and I do—I've gotta be careful."

"Oh, yeah," she murmured, still watching him and wondering why he didn't notice the steam coming out of her ears. Of course, he hadn't noticed *her* in two years. Why should he start now? "Careful."

"Seriously, Em," he said, and stood up, turning to look down at her. "Without you to talk to about this, I'd probably lose my mind."

"What's left of it," she muttered darkly.

"What?"

"Nothing."

"Right." He grinned and hooked a thumb toward her office, located at the front of the garage. "I'm going for a soda. You want one?"

"No, but you go ahead."

He nodded, then loped off toward the shop. She

watched him and, for the first time, *really* looked at him. Nice buns, she thought, startling herself. She'd never noticed Connor's behind before. Why now?

Because, she told herself, he'd just changed the rules between them. And the big dummy didn't even know it.

While the sun sizzled all around her and the damp, hot air choked in her lungs, Emma's mind raced. Oh, boy, she hadn't been this angry in years. But more than the righteous fury boiling in her blood, she was insulted...and hurt.

Just three years ago she'd allowed another man to slip beneath her radar and break her heart. Connor had, unknowingly, just joined the long list of men who had underestimated her in her life. And this time Emma wasn't going to let a guy get away with it. She was going to make him pay for this, she thought. For all the times she'd been overlooked or underappreciated. For all the men who'd considered her *less* than a woman. For all the times she'd doubted her own femininity...

Connor Reilly was going to pay.

Big-time.

A few hours later Emma was still furious, though much cooler. In her own house, she had the air conditioner set just a little above frigid, so a cup of hot tea was enjoyable at night. Usually she found a cup of tea soothing. Tonight she was afraid she'd need a lot more than tea.

Even after Connor left the garage that afternoon, she hadn't been able to stop thinking about him and about what he'd said. Anger had faded into insult and insult into bruised feelings, then circled back around to anger again.

There was only one person in the world who would understand what she was feeling. Alone at home, she set one of the last remaining two of her late mother's floral-patterned china cups on the table beside her, picked up the phone and hit the speed dial.

The phone only rang once when it was picked up and a familiar voice said "Hello."

"Mary Alice," Emma said quickly, her words tumbling over each other in her haste to be heard, "you're not going to believe this. Connor Reilly told me today that he doesn't think of me as a *woman*. I'm a 'pal.' A 'mechanic.' Remember I told you about that stupid bet he and his brothers concocted?" She didn't wait for confirmation. "Well, today he tells me that the reason he's hanging out at the garage is because he feels *safe* around me. He doesn't *want* me, so I'm neutral territory. Can you believe it? Can you actually believe he looked me dead in the eye and practically *told* me that I'm less than female?"

"Who is this?" An amused female voice interrupted her.

"Very funny." Emma smiled, in spite of her anger, then jumped up off the old, worn sofa in her family's living room and stalked to the mirror above the now-cold fireplace. "Weren't you listening to me?"

"You bet," Mary Alice said. "Heard every word. Want Tommy to call out the Recon guys, take this jerk out for you?"

Emma grinned at her own reflection. "No, but thanks." Mary Alice Flanagan, Emma's best friend since fifth grade, had married Tom Malone, a Marine, four years ago and was now currently stationed in California. It was only thanks to Mary Alice that Emma had ever discovered the mysteries of being female.

Emma's mother had died when she was an infant, and after that she'd been raised by her father. A terrific man, he'd loved his daughter to distraction, but had had no idea how to teach her to be a woman. Mary Alice's mother had filled the gap, and when they were grown, Mary Alice herself had given Emma the makeover that had helped her attract and then win the very man who'd left her heart battered and bleeding three years ago.

The two women stayed in constant touch by phone and e-mail, but this was one night Emma wished her oldest and best friend was right here in town. She needed to sit and vent.

"Okay then, if you don't want him dead, what *do* you want?" Mary Alice asked.

Emma faced the mirror and watched her own features harden. "I want him to be sorry he said that. Sorry he ever took me for granted. Heck, sorry he ever *met* me."

"You sure you want to do this?" her friend asked, and the worry was clear in her voice. "I mean, look how the thing with Tony worked out."

Emma flinched at the memory. Tony DeMarco had done more than break her heart. He'd shattered her newfound confidence and cost her the ability to trust. But that was different and she said so now. "Not the same situation," she said firmly, not sure if she was trying to convince herself or her friend. "I *loved* Tony. I don't love Connor."

"You just want to make him miserable?"

"Damn skippy."

"And your plan is…?"

"I'm gonna drive him crazy," Emma said, and she smiled at the thought of Connor Reilly groveling at her feet, begging for just a *crumb* of her attentions.

"Uh-huh."

"I'm going to make him lose that bet."

"By sleeping with him?"

"Sleep's got nothing to do with my plan," Emma said softly, and ignored the flutter of something warm and liquid rustling to life inside her.

# Two

Saint Sebastian's Catholic Church looked like a tiny castle plunked down in the middle of rural South Carolina. Made from weathered gray brick, the building's leaded windows sparkled in the morning sunlight. Huge terra-cotta pots on the front porch of the rectory, or priests' house, were filled with red, purple and blue petunias that splashed color in the dimness of the overhang. Ancient Magnolia trees stood in the yard of the church, draping the neatly clipped lawn with welcome patches of cool shade.

The church's double front doors stood open, welcoming anyone who might need to stop in and pray, but Emma drove past the church and pulled into the driveway behind the rectory.

She turned off the engine, then stepped out of the car and into the blanketing humidity of summer. The heat slapped at her, but Emma hardly noticed. She'd grown up in the South and she was used to the heat that regularly made short work of tourists.

Besides, if she was looking to avoid the heat, she could have stayed at the shop, in the air-conditioned splendor of her office, and had one of her mechanics drive Father Liam's aging sedan back to him. But she'd wanted the opportunity to talk to Connor's older brother.

Ever since her enlightening conversation with Connor the day before, Emma'd been fuming. And thinking. A combustible combination. She'd lain awake half the night, torn between insult and anger and even now, she wasn't sure which was the stronger emotion churning inside her.

She'd thought that maybe talking to Liam might help sort things out. Now that she was here, though, she didn't have a clue what to say to the man.

Muttering darkly, she headed past the small basketball court in front of the garage, down the rosebush-lined driveway and around to the front door.

She knocked, and almost instantly the door was opened by a tall, older woman with graying red hair and sharp green eyes. Her mouth was pinched into its perpetual frown. "Miss Jacobsen."

"Hi, Mrs. Hannigan," Emma said, ignoring the woman's usual lack of welcome. Practically a stereotypical housekeeper, she was straight out of an old Gothic novel. So, Emma never took her grim sense of disapproval personally. Mrs. Hannigan didn't like anybody.

Stepping into the house, she glanced around and smiled at the polished dark wood paneling, the faded but still colorful braided rugs and the tiny, diamond-shaped slices of sunlight on the gleaming wood floor. "I brought Father Liam's car back. Just want to give him the keys and the bill."

"He's in the library," the housekeeper said, already turning for the hall leading back down the house toward the kitchen. "You go in, I'll bring tea."

"That's okay—" Horrified, Emma spoke up quickly, trying to head the woman off. Everyone in Baywater knew enough to say no to Mrs. Hannigan's tea. But it was too late. The housekeeper ignored Emma's protest and strode down the hallway, filled with purpose, and Emma knew there would be no getting out of having to drink the world's worst tea just to be polite.

Grumbling to herself, she crossed the hall, opened the door into the library and paused, waiting for the young priest to notice her. It didn't take long.

Father Liam Reilly set aside the book he was reading, stood up and smiled at her, and Emma had to remind herself that he was a dedicated priest. As she was sure *every* female was forced to do when face to face with Liam.

As tall as his brothers, he was every bit as gorgeous, too. His black hair, longer than the triplets' military cuts, was thick and wavy and his deep-blue eyes were fringed by long black lashes any woman would envy. His generous mouth was usually curved in a smile that set people immediately at ease, and today was no exception.

"Emma! I'm guessing your arrival means you were able to save my car again?" He crossed to her and dropped one arm around her shoulder, leading her to a pair of overstuffed chairs near a fireplace that held, instead of flaming logs, a copper bucket filled with summer roses.

"I brought it back from the brink again, Liam," she said, and handed him the bill she pulled out of her back pocket before taking the seat he offered. "But it's on life support. You're going to need a new one soon."

He grinned, then glanced at the bill and winced. "I know," he said, lifting his gaze to hers. "But there's always a more important use for the money. And Connor's promised to rebuild the engine when he gets a chance, so I'll wait him out."

*Connor.*

The very man she wanted to talk about. But now that she was here, she really didn't know what to say. How could she tell a *priest* that she wanted to kill his brother?

"Something wrong?" Liam asked, sitting down across from her and leaning forward, elbows braced on his knees.

"What makes you ask that?"

He smiled. "Because the minute I said the name Connor, your face froze and your eyes caught fire."

"I guess poker's not my game, huh?"

"No." He shook his head, reached out, tapped the back of one of her hands and asked, "So, want to talk?"

Emma opened her mouth, but they were interrupted. She wasn't sure if that was a good thing or not.

"Tea, Father," Mrs. Hannigan announced as she bustled into the room carrying a wide tray loaded with a pitcher of a murky brown liquid, two tall glasses filled with ice and a plate of cookies.

"Oh," Liam said with heartfelt sincerity, "you really didn't have to do that, Mrs. Hannigan."

"No trouble." She set down the tray, dusted her palms together, then turned on her heel and marched out of the room with near military precision.

"We have to drink it," Liam said on a sigh as he reached for the pitcher.

"I know." Emma braced herself as she watched him pour what looked like mud into the glasses.

"She's a good woman," Liam said, lifting his own glass and eyeing it dubiously. "Though I can't imagine why the concept of tea escapes her."

Emma decided to get it over with and took a hearty swig. She gulped it down before it could stick in her throat, then set the glass back on the tray and coughed a little before speaking again. "So about Connor…"

"Right." Liam gagged a little at the tea, set the glass down and shuddered. "What'd he do?"

Intrigued, Emma asked, "How did you know he did anything?"

"Something put that flash of anger in your eyes, Emma."

"Okay, yeah. You're right." She jumped up from the chair that was big enough and soft enough to swallow her whole and started walking. Nowhere in particular, she just felt as though she needed to move. "He did do something, well, *said* something and it made me so mad, Liam, I almost punched him and then I thought he wouldn't even understand why I was hitting him and then *that* made me even more mad, which even I could hardly believe, because honestly I was never so mad in my life and he didn't even have a clue. You know?"

She was walking in circles, and Liam kept his head swiveling, to keep up with her, following her progress around the room and trying to keep up with the rambling fury of her words.

"So, would you hate me, too, if I said I don't have the slightest idea what you're talking about?"

Emma blew out a breath and stopped in front of the wide windows overlooking the shady front lawn. The scent of the roses in the cold hearth mingled with the homey scent of lemon oil clinging to the gleaming woodwork. Outside, a slight wind tugged at the leaves of the magnolias and two kids, oblivious to the heat, raced past the church, baseball bats on their shoulders.

"He's an idiot." Emma turned and looked at him. "Connor, I mean."

"True," Liam admitted and gave her a smile that took the edge off her anger. "In fact, all of my brothers are idiots—" he caught himself and corrected "—maybe not Brian anymore since he wised up in time to keep Tina in his life. But Connor and Aidan?" He nodded. "Idiots. Still, in their defense, they're under a lot of...*pressure,* right now."

"You mean the bet?" Emma asked.

Liam blinked. "You know about it?"

"It's practically all Connor's talked about for the last month."

"Is that right?" Liam smiled again, wider this time. "Driving him crazy, is it?"

Emma grinned at him, despite the bubbles of anger still simmering inside her. "You're really enjoying this, aren't you?"

"I shouldn't be, should I?"

"I don't know," Emma said, her smile fading just a little, "okay, you're a priest, but you *are* still a Reilly."

"Guilty as charged," Liam admitted. "And this Reilly wants to know what Connor did that upset you so much."

"He dismissed me."

"Excuse me?"

Emma shrugged, as if she could shift what felt like a load off her shoulders, then shoved both hands into the pockets of her jeans. Blowing out a breath, she realized that it was just a little harder than she'd thought it would be to talk about this. Saying it all out loud only made it harsher and made her remember the stupid smile in Connor's eyes when he told her she was a "pal."

Gritting her teeth, Emma got a grip on her anger and muttered thickly, "He actually told me that he didn't want me, so I was safe to be around."

Liam groaned. "He really is an idiot."

"Yeah, well." Feeling the sting of Connor's words again, Emma turned her head and looked out the window, focusing on the gnarled trunk of the closest magnolia tree. She should just be mad, but there was an undeniable sting of hurt jabbing at her, too. And it was that niggling pain that bothered her the most. She hadn't let a man close enough to actually *hurt* her in three years. The fact that Connor could do it without even trying infuriated her.

"He's going to be sorry," she whispered, more as a solemn promise to herself than to Liam.

"Emma?"

She wouldn't look at him. How could she? She heard the concern in his voice, and though she appreciated it, she didn't need it. She'd be fine. Just as she'd always been. And once Connor had been taught a *very* costly lesson, things would go back to the way they should be. "I'm going to see to it he loses that bet, Liam."

He sighed and she heard him stand up and walk toward her. "Not that I wouldn't be pleased if the church got a new roof," Liam said when he stopped beside her. "But I feel I ought to caution you."

"About?" She slanted him a look.

Shaking his head, Liam said softly, "Sometimes the best-laid traps can backfire, Emma. They can spring shut on the one who set the trap in the first place."

Not if the trapper was careful.

"Don't worry about me, Liam," she said firmly. "I'll be fine."

"Uh-huh," he said, and reached out to turn her face toward him. "But you and Connor have been friends for a long time."

"So?" She didn't mean to sound so much like a cranky child. But she couldn't seem to help it. The fact that they *had* been friends was the very thing that had made this whole situation so infuriating.

"*So,*" he said, "it's not that far a fall from friendship to love."

Emma laughed and shook her head. "Sorry for laughing, Liam. But trust me, there's no chance of that."

Number one, she wasn't interested in loving anybody. She'd tried that once and she still had the emotional bruises to prove it. And Connor wasn't looking for love either. Heck, if anything, he was trying to avoid women altogether. And clearly, she told herself, her spine straightening and her chin lifting, if he *were* to go looking for love…he wouldn't be looking at her. Nope. No danger here.

Still chuckling, she turned and headed for the door. "I've got to get back to the garage," she said. "And don't worry about giving me a ride back. It's only a few blocks. I could use the walk."

At the door, she stopped and turned back to look at him again. Father Liam was watching her with a concerned expression on his handsome face.

"Don't look so worried," she quipped. "I'm going to help you get that new roof."

"A new roof's not worth a broken heart, Emma."

If something inside her shivered, she ignored it. He meant well, but he didn't understand. This wasn't about making Connor love her. This was about making Connor want her, and then leaving him flat.

This was about payback.

"Hearts are *not* involved here, Liam."

Still worried, Liam watched her go. "For your sake, I hope you're right."

Two days later Connor couldn't stand his own company any longer.

He'd been avoiding his usual hangouts—except for Jacobsen's Garage—but Emma hadn't had much time to talk to him in the last couple of days. He might have thought that she was avoiding him, but that didn't make any sense at all.

To fill his time, he'd spent a few hours working in his mother's garden, played basketball with Liam and had even mooched a meal from Brian and Tina. But, Connor thought, as good a cook as his sister-in-law was, he just couldn't take another evening over there. Not with the way Brian and Tina were all over each other.

It was hell to be jealous of a married man.

But there it was.

"I think going without sex is killing off brain cells," he muttered, and shut off his car's engine. Instantly the air conditioner died and the temperature in the car started to climb.

Summer nights weren't much cooler than summer days and the humidity was enough to make a grown man weep. He stared through the windshield at the Off Duty Bar and told himself if he was smart, he'd fire up the engine, turn the car around and drive back to his empty apartment.

But damn it, temptation of women or not, Connor wanted a couple of hours of listening to music, drinking a beer and talking to his friends.

"I can do this," he assured himself as he opened the car door and stepped out into the sultry summer air. Music, loud but muffled, floated to him on the way-too-slight breeze and the scent of jasmine, coming from the bushes growing at the edge of the parking lot, was thick and sweet.

Connor slammed the car door, punched the alarm button until the car horn beeped, then headed for the front door. As he walked closer, a couple left the building, the man's arm wrapped tightly around his woman's shoulders as he dropped a kiss on her hair.

Connor groaned and seriously considered turning back while there was still time. But the lure of air-conditioning, cold beer and some conversation was just too strong. He grabbed the silver bar in the center of the door and gave it a yank. The door flew open, music slapped at him, and the scent of perfume, beer and cigarette smoke welcomed him.

He stepped into the dimly lit room and nodded greetings as he made his way to the bar. Signaling the bartender, Connor said, "Beer. Draft." He slapped a bill on the bar top and when his drink was ready, he lifted it and took a long pull.

The icy froth soothed him as it slid down his throat, and he shifted his gaze to take in the room. The bar itself was old. Probably fifty years at least. The walls were painted battleship gray and the furniture was scarred. From the open, beamed ceiling, hung memorabilia of the corps. Vintage helmets, bayonets in frayed scabbards, and even a ceremonial sword, belonging to the current owner, a retired Sergeant Major. The whole place was designed to make a military man feel welcome. A Marine, most of all.

There were pool tables at one end of the main room, and on the opposite end, a dozen round tables were lined up in a wide circle, so that the middle of the ring could be used for dancing. The jukebox, which looked older than Connor, blasted out current rock along with some of the classics.

Most of the regulars at the Off Duty were Marines. Winding down after a day of work or just stopping in for a cold one before going home. Of course, there were also a few civilians and more than a few women.

Not that Connor was noticing.

Then the crowd shifted. His hand tightened on the glass of beer. Through the gap in the people milling around the bar, he had an all-too-clear view of a tall blonde in a skirt short enough to be just barely legal.

She was bending over the pool table, lining up a shot.

Connor's mouth went dry.

Her long, blond hair hung in a honey-colored curtain down to the middle of her back. As she tipped her head to one side, that fall of hair shifted, off her shoulders and his gaze was caught by the way the overhead light picked out streaks of sun-kissed hair, brighter than the rest. She wore a pale-blue tank top that looked as if it had been glued onto her body, and the tiny denim skirt, just covering her behind, hitched even higher as she leaned farther over the pool table. Her shapely legs looked smooth and tanned and about three miles long. She wore black, sky-high heels on her small feet, and her ankles looked as fragile as her thighs looked sexy.

Sexy?

The woman *oozed* sex.

His fingers squeezed the glass of beer until he wouldn't have been surprised to feel it shatter like spun sugar in his grasp. Scraping one hand across his face, he inhaled sharply and watched, spellbound, as she lifted her right foot and rubbed it slowly against her left calf.

Need spiked.

His body went instantly hard.

His breath shuddered and his heartbeat staggered.

He watched one of the guys closest to her, lean in and whisper something, and Connor wanted to grab the guy and pitch him through a window.

Okay, *breathe*.

He sucked in air and told himself that he was only reacting like this because of his recent dry spell.

But it was more.

There was something about her.

Something that called to him from all the way across the room. Something that made a man want to toss her over his shoulder and carry her off to a cave where he could have her, over and over again. Where he could listen to her moan and taste her sighs.

He took another gulp of beer, hoping the icy drink would put out some of the fire. But he knew better. Damn it, he never should have come in here.

The blonde straightened up slowly, then hitched one hip higher than the other as she laughed. That tight, short skirt of hers hugged her behind. She shook her long blond hair back from her face, and Connor was captivated, watching the thick, wavy fall of blond shift and dance around her.

He swallowed hard.

Then she tipped her head back and playfully patted the other guy's chest.

Connor dropped his beer.

The glass shattered at his feet, splashing ice cold beer on everyone close by.

He didn't notice.

He couldn't take his eyes off the blond with the body made for sex.

*"Emma?"*

# Three

**E**ven over the pounding rhythm of the jukebox, Emma heard the glass shatter.

But then, her ears were attuned to everything. She'd seen Connor walk into the bar—which was exactly why she'd maneuvered herself to the end of the pool table. She'd even opted to take a *lousy* shot, because she knew *exactly* what kind of picture she'd make, leaning over the pool table.

Nerves hit her hard and fast. Her stomach spun, and the edges of her vision got a little foggy, but she could deal with that. Had to deal with it. Too late now to change her plan.

Smiling up at the guy she'd just beaten at pool, she ignored the sensation of Connor's gaze boring into her back. "That's twenty bucks you owe me, Mike. Want to go double or nothing?"

The tall Marine smiled down at her as he handed over a twenty-dollar bill. "How about you let me buy you a drink instead?"

"How about you take off?" Connor's voice was nothing more than a low growl.

Emma shifted a look at him and had to force herself not to smile at the stunned-to-his-toes expression on his face. Good. She definitely had his attention.

"Connor," she said, in mock surprise. "I didn't see you come in."

Viciously he rubbed the back of his neck, then let his hand drop to his side. "Yeah, well. I sure as hell saw *you.*"

"Friend of yours?"

Emma glanced back at the man she'd just beaten twice at pool. Tall and good-looking, any other night she just might be interested. Tonight, though, every thought was centered on Connor. But Mike didn't look too pleased at the idea of sharing.

They were attracting a small crowd, drawn no doubt by the bristling testosterone in the air. Emma wanted to shake her head at the ridiculousness of it, but there was a small part of her enjoying the whole show.

After all, she spent most of her time being just what Connor had called her. One of the guys. A pal. Well, she'd been underestimated most of her life. True, she'd probably played into it by never bothering to dress the part of "female." But she'd always figured she shouldn't have to. A woman who was a successful business owner should be accepted on her own terms without having to stand in killer high heels and skirts so short she felt a breeze *way* too high up.

"Emma," Mike said, bringing her up out of her thoughts with a jerk. "You know this guy?"

"Oh, yes," she said, sending another look to Connor and really enjoying seeing him watch the other guy through narrowed eyes. "Connor and I are old *friends.*"

"And we need to talk," Connor said, not bothering to take the warning out of his voice as he faced the other Marine. "So why don't you get lost?"

"Yeah?" Mike snarled. "I don't remember inviting you over."

Connor's chin went up, Mike stiffened and curled his hands into fists, and Emma suddenly felt as though she were in the middle of a special on that cable channel about animals. The men were like two bull elephants about to butt heads.

And in spite of the anger she still felt toward Connor, a purely female spurt of delight shot through her—which she quickly shot down. Seriously, two men go caveman and woman reverts right along with them. Must be contagious.

Stepping in between them, Emma smiled up at Mike Whatever-his-last-name-was and said, "It's okay. I do need to talk to Connor so..." She let her sentence trail off and shrugged an apology.

He didn't like it, but he moved away, rejoining his

friends at the bar. Connor glared after him, then shifted his gaze back to Emma.

With a calm she wasn't quite feeling, she folded the twenty-dollar bill she'd just won and tucked it into her bra—the push-up kind that gave her more cleavage than God had ever gifted her with. And she didn't miss Connor's gaze following the action.

A swirl of something hot and thick simmered within, and she told herself it was purely a female re-action to a male stare of appreciation. Although, she hadn't exactly been panting when Mike was giving her the once-over.

*Doesn't matter.*

All that mattered was that her plan was working.

She smiled to herself and rubbed the tip of her cue stick with a square of chalk. Then, setting it aside, she pursed her lips and blew gently on the tip. Con-nor swallowed hard.

This is just *fun*, Emma thought.

"So," she said, tipping her head to one side so that her hair fell around her like a gold curtain, "what'd you want to talk about?"

He snorted and swept his gaze up and down her. "You're kidding, right?"

She leaned one hip against the pool table, while she idly stroked her fingers up and down the cue stick. "Is there a problem?"

"A *problem?*" Connor's eyes bugged out and his mouth worked a time or two, as if he was trying to speak but just couldn't convince the words to cooperate. Finally he got a grip on himself, leaned in toward her and said in a strained hush, "Damn it, Emma, *look* at you. When you were bent over that pool table, I could see clear to—"

She raised one eyebrow and hid the delighted smile she felt inside. "Clear to *where,* Connor?"

He straightened up. "Doesn't matter." He inhaled sharply. "What *does* matter is that every guy in here is looking, too."

Okay, there was just a tiny stirring of uneasiness. She'd *wanted* Connor to get an eyeful, and she'd known going in that she might attract some attention from other guys. But the thought of a roomful of Marines scoping her out gave her a chill that wasn't quite the thrill she might have guessed. If anything, she felt a little...*outnumbered.*

But she wasn't going to let Connor know it.

"And how is this any of your business?" she asked.

"Well," he started, then stammered to a stop. He glanced around, giving the evil eye to one guy sidling a little too close for his comfort, then shifted a glare back at her. "We're *friends,* Em," he said. "I'm just trying to look out for you. That's all."

"That's the only reason you came over here, then?" She didn't believe him for a minute. There was a flash of something dark and dangerous in his eyes and it didn't have a thing to do with feelings for his *pal.*

"Why else?"

Okay, fine. They'd play this out. She could go

along. In fact, this worked out better for her. The longer he tried to hold out against her, the harder she'd make it for him.

Pushing away from the pool table, she picked up her cue stick, then ran the tips of her fingers along the top edge of her tank top, as if she were hot. She didn't miss Connor's gaze snapping right to where she wanted him to be looking.

"Well, thanks, Connor," she said, licking her lips slowly, provocatively. "I appreciate the concern."

He gritted his teeth, and she watched a muscle in his jaw tick.

"No problem. In fact," he added, "if you're ready to leave, I'll just take you home. Make sure you're okay."

Emma smiled up at him despite the urge to smack him over the head with her cue stick. Instead she laid one hand on his chest and felt the drumbeat of his heart beneath her palm. "That's so sweet," she said softly. "But no, thanks, I'm not ready to leave yet."

"You're not   "

"Tell you what," she said, sliding past him in a move that put her between his rock-hard body and the edge of the pool table. As she moved, she heard him hiss in a breath. Good. "Now that you've scared off my playing partner, you ready to take me on instead?"

He scowled. "Take you on?"

She snapped her fingers in front of his glassy eyes. "Pool, Reilly. You want to play me a game of pool?"

"Right. Pool. Sure." He scrubbed both hands over his face, then looked at her again and blinked as if trying to clear blurry vision. "It'd be better if we just left and—"

"Oh, you go ahead," she said, letting her gaze slide around the room, as if she were considering picking a different challenger from the men in the bar. "I can find someone else to play."

"I'll bet," he muttered darkly. "Look, Emma, I just don't think you should be hanging out here—not tonight. Not the way you look—"

One blond eyebrow lifted again, and slowly she hitched one hip higher than the other and tapped the toe of her shoe against the floor. Around them, people laughed and talked and a handful of couples danced on a small square of unoccupied floor. She paid no attention to any of it.

"What?" she asked. "I look what, exactly? Good? Bad?"

He scowled at her. "Different."

She turned to hide her smile and offered herself a small internal *whoop* of congratulation. Mission accomplished. Connor Reilly had taken notice. In fact, if he'd noticed any harder, he'd be standing in a puddle of drool. A sense of power swept through her, and Emma hugged it close.

A heady sensation for a *pal*.

She picked up the triangle-shaped rack hanging on the side of the pool table, then set it down in position on the green felt. Not even looking at him, she said, "I wasn't born in coveralls, you know."

"Sure. I know that," he said, and reached into the

corner pocket to pull out a handful of the striped and solid balls. "It's just…"

Emma sighed and muttered under her breath. Okay, she'd thought to surprise him, but this was ridiculous. It was as if he were staring at a dog who'd suddenly learned to talk. How was she going to seduce the man—make him lose that stupid bet—if she couldn't get him to move past *stunned* into *hunger?*

She straightened up and moved closer to him. His gaze went right to the top of her scoop-necked tank top and stayed there. Her breasts looked high and full, thanks to the "miracle" bra that was currently strangling her. And Connor was certainly appreciating the view.

And that's what she'd wanted, right?

"Look," she said, "I want to play pool. If you don't want to, I'll just ask Mike, or one of these other guys, if he wants to go another round and—"

"Leave him and anybody else out of this," Connor muttered thickly, lifting his gaze to hers. "I'll play."

Now, a girl could take that one of two ways. Play *what* exactly? Pool? Or something else, entirely? For the moment, she'd go with pool. "Twenty bucks a round. Eight ball."

"You're on."

"Then," she said, walking past him to circle the table and head for the opposite end, "as the challenger, you rack 'em."

"Yes, ma'am."

* * *

Connor couldn't take his eyes off her.

Damn it, who would have guessed that little Emma Jacobsen was packing concealed weapons?

And man, she had weapons to spare.

The tops of her breasts pushed teasingly against the edge of her tiny tank top. Her hips swayed when she walked and the hem of that incredibly short skirt just barely managed to cover the gateway to paradise. And her legs. God, her legs.

He dropped one of the billiard balls and had to bend down to snatch it up off the floor. Which gave him much too good a view of those amazing legs as she walked away from him. And why had he never noticed the sweet curve of her behind?

How could he have missed it?

His whole body was stiff as a board. He felt hot and eager and pushed to the very edge of self-control. Damn it, it had been a mistake to come here. He'd known it before and he was sure of it now. But if he hadn't, he might never have seen this side of Emma.

The very side that was making it an effort to walk. He suddenly wished that his jeans were a hell of a lot baggier.

And even as he thought it, he straightened up, his grip on the fallen billiard ball tight enough to crush it to dust. *This is Emma,* he reminded himself. *Good old Emma.*

Pal.

Buddy.

He shifted his gaze to her and felt his throat close

up. Her blue eyes looked wider tonight. Her mouth looked edible. Her tanned, smooth skin was the color of warm honey and looked just as lickable.

Oh, man.

She was watching him with a curious expression on her face and he really couldn't blame her. Hell, they'd been hanging out together for a couple of years now and he'd never stuttered around her before. Just like he'd never taken the time to notice that her breasts were just the right size to fill a man's palm.

Damn it.

She held her cue stick in her left hand. Idly, she slid her fingers up and down the slim, polished wood, trailing her touch delicately enough to drive him insane by wondering how those fingers would feel on *him.*

"Man, get a grip, Reilly." His voice was thick and his muttered whisper was soft enough to be buried beneath the onslaught of rock music pouring into the room. At least, he hoped it had been.

He really didn't want Emma knowing that he was getting hard just watching her.

*It's just the bet.*

That's all it was.

He was hard up.

Frustrated.

Walking the fine edge of sanity.

But man, she looked good.

"How long's it take to rack some balls?" she asked.

Connor winced and shot her a quick look. "A little patience goes a long way."

She laughed and the deep, throaty, full sound of it, rippled over the conversations in the bar and danced to the rhythm of the music. It seemed to reach for him and grab him by the throat.

"You?" she asked. "Patient?"

Her fingers were still caressing the cue stick and he had to force himself to look away. But meeting her gaze wasn't much safer. Had her eyes always been that color of blue? Sort of summer skyish? He gritted his teeth.

"I can be patient when I have to be," he countered. Like now. It had been a long month. The stupid bet with his brothers was making him crazy. But he was patient—even if Emma didn't think so. And he'd make it through the next two months.

As long as she didn't bend over again.

"Yeah?" She tilted her head, and that fall of hair swung out past her shoulders. "How are you at pool?"

He lifted the rack off the triangle of balls, hung it on the hook at the end of the table and forced a nonchalant shrug. "Take your best shot and let's find out."

She nodded slowly. "Twenty bucks a game."

"High stakes."

"What's the matter?" she asked, a smile tugging at the corners of her mouth. "Scared?"

Well, that helped. His dignity won out over his hormones. "Hell, no. I can take you."

"Really?" she said softly. "And just *where* did you plan on taking me?"

She didn't wait for a reply. Instead, she bent over

the table, lined up her cue stick and drew it back and forth between her fingers while she aimed her shot.

Unfortunately, this gave Connor *way* too much time to appreciate the view of her breasts, practically spilling out of her tank top.

His body went to DefCon 2.

And he suddenly knew *just* where he'd like to take her.

A back room.

A flat surface.

On the damn pool table.

*Crap.* He rubbed his face and damn near slapped himself. He wanted *Emma.* Now. More than he could ever remember wanting anything else in his life.

The only thing that stopped him was he was pretty sure it wouldn't have worked. Just because he was acting like a slobbering horn dog didn't mean she was feeling the same thing. And the only thing worse than falling off the wagon and losing the bet would be trying to lose the bet and having Emma tell him thanks but no thanks.

She took her shot, and the triangle of balls scattered across the green felt surface. She looked up at him and grinned, and Connor's breath caught in his throat.

"You sure you're willing to risk the twenty bucks?" she asked, her voice teasing.

"I'm not afraid of a challenge," he countered, leaning both hands on the cherry wood edge of the table. "How about you?"

"Oh, don't you worry about me, Connor. Trust me, I'm up to the challenge."

"Yeah?" he asked. "And after I've won your twenty bucks, then what'll we play for?"

Emma lined up her next shot, then paused to slant him a look. "Oh, I'm sure we'll think of something."

# Four

Emma Jacobsen was driving him over the edge and damned if she didn't seem to be enjoying the ride.

Connor lost two games of pool and couldn't even resent the laughter from the handful of people gathered around to watch the competition. How could he? Hell, if he'd been watching, he'd have been laughing his butt off at the poor guy getting worked by the petite woman in the tank top.

But damned if he could help himself.

How was a man supposed to concentrate on a game when he kept getting distracted by a woman's breasts? Or her legs? Or her laughter? Or the way she walked?

Damn it.

Emma crossed to the wall and set her cue stick into the rack before slowly maneuvering through the crowd to his side. Holding out her hand, she waited for him to hand over his last twenty.

"You were using secret weapons," he said and dropped the bill into her hand, too wary of actually *touching* her. Though the thought of his fingers brushing her palm sent a jolt of heat darting through him, he figured he shouldn't risk it. Hell, he wasn't sure he'd be able to *stop* touching her if he got started.

"Is that right?" she asked, and grinned up at him. Her smile packed a hell of a punch. Something else he'd never noticed. Emma had smiled at him maybe hundreds of times over the past couple of years. Why had it never hit him just what a great mouth she had? What…had he been going through his life blind or something?

"Oh, yeah." Connor forced the words past the hard knot in his throat. "Trust me when I say you weren't fighting fair."

Shaking her head, she laughed and said, "And here I thought I just played way better than you."

"Another match another time," he promised. As long as she was wrapped up in an Eskimo jacket.

"I'm always ready for a challenge." She smiled and tucked the twenty-dollar bill into the dip of her cleavage. He watched it disappear and his mouth went dry.

Behind them, a couple of guys moved in to take over the pool table. Emma stared up at him for a long minute or two, and Connor's brain tried to kick into gear. He had to say something. Something to convince—if not her, then at least himself—that he wasn't a slobbering moron.

But apparently his mind was taking the night off.

In those sky-high heels of hers, she was taller than usual. Her mouth was close enough to kiss and tempting enough to make him want to risk it. He could almost taste her and that thought splintered inside him until he had to curl his hands into fists to keep from reaching for her.

Damn it.

This was *Emma*.

Has to be the bet, he told himself.

Then she spoke and he listened up. Her voice was soft, so he had to strain to hear her over the clash of music and conversation. Not to mention the thunderous pounding of his own heart.

"You're staring at me."

"No, I'm not." Stupid.

"Okay," she allowed, a smirk curving her lips. "You're staring at the wall behind me and I'm just in the way?"

He scraped one hand over his face, hoping to stir himself out of the sexual coma he'd slipped into. Didn't help much. "Sorry. Thinking."

Yeah, thinking about tossing her onto the pool table and peeling her out of that tank top and skirt. Geez, he could almost feel her amazing legs wrapped around his hips.

DefCon 1.

He was definitely in too deep here.

"Uh-huh," Emma said, with a shake of her head that told him she wasn't buying the whole "lost in thought" excuse. Already turning, she said, "Well, it's been fun, Connor, but I've gotta be going."

She was leaving.

He should be grateful.

He wasn't.

"What's your hurry?" he asked, voice tight.

She stopped and looked up at him.

He mentally scrambled for something to say. Something that would convince her to stay for a while. He wasn't finished torturing himself. Wasn't finished being amazed by the surprise that was Emma.

Blowing out a breath, he said, "I'd offer to buy you a beer, but somebody just won all my cash."

A quicksilver grin flashed across her face and was gone again in an instant. "So if I was a good sport, I'd buy *you* a beer?"

"Something like that." Anything, he told himself. He just wasn't ready yet for this time with her to be over. Wasn't even sure why, but he knew he wanted to be with her. Even over all the other scents colliding in the air of the bar, he could almost taste the scent clinging to her alone. It was fresh and citrusy and reminded him of long summer nights under star-filled skies.

And he couldn't quite believe it was Emma Jacobsen making him feel all these things. Maybe that was why he didn't want her to leave yet, he told himself, grasping for a reason, *any* reason. Maybe he had to prove to himself that it wasn't Emma herself affecting him. That it could have been any woman at this point in the bet. That he was just a hormone-plagued, needy Marine, and any good-looking woman could have been the last straw on this particular camel's back.

No doubt about it, either, she was real good-looking. Up, down or sideways, Emma had something that was making him reel.

"Sorry," she was saying. "Work tomorrow, so I'm heading out."

She turned and weaved through the crowd, moving for the front door. Guys she passed craned their necks for a better view. Connor was surprised there wasn't a river of drool running through the bar. As he watched them watch her, he felt the sudden, driving urge to slam all their heads together and let them fall.

Where the hell did they get off watching Emma?

A couple of long seconds ticked by before he reacted. But then he was moving fast, pushing past the people in his way, as if they were deliberately trying to separate him from Emma. He caught up with her just outside.

The scent of jasmine was thick and sweet in the hot summer air. The silence, after the door swung closed behind him, was almost startling after the prolonged exposure to blaring music. And in the relative quiet, he heard her steps, crunching in the gravel of the parking lot. Instinctively he followed.

She spun around, right hand raised and fisted, with keys jutting out from between her fingers.

"Whoa!" Connor held both hands up in mock surrender.

Emma sighed and let her hand fall. "Darn it, Connor, you *scared* me."

"Sorry, sorry." He hadn't thought about it. Hadn't considered the fact that she might get a little spooked having someone chase her into the parking lot.

In fact he'd *never* stopped to think about Emma that way and suddenly, he realized that she must cross lots of dark parking lots. What about at night, when she closed up her shop and she was alone? And he wondered why he suddenly felt as though he wanted to be the guy protecting her.

*Oh, man.*

This just kept getting worse and worse.

"What do you want, Connor?"

He lifted her right hand, ignoring the heat that spread from her hand to his and up his arm. Silently he examined the keys she held primed between her fingers. "You were ready for trouble, weren't you?"

"Uh, *yeah.*" She pulled her hand free and released her tight grip on the keys. "A smart woman pays attention and doesn't take chances. So, why'd you follow me out here, Connor? Forget to tell me something?"

"No," he blurted, and took her elbow in a firm

grip. She felt warm and soft and, damn it, way too good. "I just thought I'd walk you to your car."

She glanced down at his hand on her arm and he wondered if she felt the same sweeping sensation of warmth that had jolted through him at first contact.

"That's not necessary," she assured him, pointing off to her left. "My car's right there."

He glanced in that direction and spotted her small, two-door, silver sedan about thirty feet away, parked directly beneath one of the light poles. Smart, he thought. Emma'd always been smart.

Then he shifted his gaze back to the sky-blue eyes still watching him. "Fine. You don't need me to do this. But it's necessary for me."

"I can take care of myself, Connor. I always have."

"I know." He'd never thought about it until tonight, but now he wondered why the hell he hadn't. Emma'd always been his friend. Someone he could shoot the breeze with as easily as he could one of the guys on base. He'd never really stopped to think of her as being female.

But looking at her tonight, he couldn't imagine thinking of her as anything else ever again.

"Humor me."

"Why should I?"

He smiled. This was the Emma he knew. Stubborn, ready to argue at the drop of a hat, unwilling to accept help if she figured she could handle something—and she *always* figured she could handle anything.

"Because," he said, smoothing his fingers over

her elbow, enjoying the slide of skin to skin, "you just beat me into the ground in front of about a hundred witnesses. Every Marine I know is going to be giving me hell about losing a game of pool to you."

"*Three* games, but who's counting," she corrected.

"*Two*," he said and leaned closer, "and *I'm* counting."

"Of course you are." Connor'd always been competitive. Which was why he'd gotten himself involved in that silly bet in the first place.

*The bet.*

The reason she was here, dressed like…well, she didn't really want to think about what she was dressed like. She'd spent most of the evening feeling *really* exposed. At least, until Connor had arrived. Then she'd pretty much just felt warm.

Emma inhaled slowly, deeply and told herself to get a grip. But it wasn't easy. The feel of Connor's hand at her elbow was swamping her brain with way too many emotions and too few clear thoughts.

She'd thought this was going to be easy.

Work him into a frenzy, seduce him, then tell him how she'd tricked him into losing the bet with his brothers.

She hadn't expected that *she* would be having trouble keeping focused.

But having his heated gaze locked on her body for the past two hours had churned her up so much that it was hard to remember to breathe. In fact, she hadn't taken an easy breath at all until the minute she'd stepped out of the bar and started across the parking lot.

Connor coming up behind her and scaring her out of five years of her life hadn't helped anything, either. But now he was here. So close. Close enough that she could look up into his eyes and see her own reflection staring back at her.

"So, are you going to let me play white knight?" he asked softly, "Or are you going to force me to follow you at a distance to make sure you're safe?"

Something inside her softened and then toughened up again. Sure, it was nice having someone care enough to make sure she got to her car safely. But if she'd wanted, or needed, an escort, one of the bouncers would have walked her out. The fact that Connor was all of a sudden acting like Sir Walter Raleigh or something was both flattering and infuriating.

She hadn't missed the fact that he'd only treated her like a girl when she was dressed as *he* thought a girl should be. If she was smart, she'd play along, keep reeling him into the fact that for the night, she was a soft, helpless female type.

But she just couldn't do it.

"First tell me something."

"What?"

"How come you never offered to walk me to my car before tonight?"

"You know," he admitted, lifting one hand to brush the side of his head, "I was just asking myself the same thing."

She watched him, admiring the strain of his black USMC T-shirt across his broad, muscled chest. "And did you get an answer?"

He straightened up again, and looked down into her eyes, pinning her gaze with his until Emma saw that his deep, ocean-blue eyes were churning with emotions she'd never expected to see.

"Only one," he muttered, taking a firmer grip on her elbow and steering her across the dark lot. The lights rimming the lot shimmered in pools of brightness splashed across the shadows.

"Which was?" She hurried her steps to keep up with his much-longer legs.

He stopped and looked at her. "I'm an idiot."

She smiled. "I can accept that."

Standing in one of the pools of light thrown from overhead, Connor's face was in shadow, but she felt him watching her anyway.

"You surprised me tonight, Em," he said, and his voice sounded softer than the breeze that drifted past them.

Her stomach did a slow spin. "Why's that?"

He shrugged. "I just never thought of you as—"

If he came right out and said, "I never thought of you as a girl," again, Emma might just have to punch him.

"As what?"

He paused, then seemed to catch himself. He took a step back, shook his head and muttered, "A pool player."

Disappointment curled in the pit of her stomach. He could have said, sexy, or hot stuff or gorgeous. But, no. Apparently, the shock was still too much for him. Well, fine. So she wouldn't be seducing him on the first try. She had time. She'd get him into bed yet.

"Live and learn," she said, and stepped past him to open her car door. She slid inside, rolled down the window and looked up at him. "See you, Connor."

"Right. See you."

She put the car in Reverse and pulled out of her parking space. As she slipped the gear shift into Drive, she looked in the rearview mirror to see Connor, standing where she'd left him, still watching after her.

The fact that she really wanted to go back and kiss him meant absolutely nothing.

"It's *Emma*, for crying out loud." Connor snatched the basketball thrown at him, then dribbled it absentmindedly.

"You gonna play or what?" Aidan ran up to him, grabbed the ball away from him, turned and made a jump shot, sending the basketball through the hoop.

"Maybe he's got something else on his mind," Brian said, wiping sweat off his face with his forearm.

"What about Emma?" Liam asked, grabbing the ball in rebound and bouncing it back down the driveway behind the rectory.

Connor looked at his older brother and wondered how in the hell he could explain what had happened to him two nights ago. Hell, he still couldn't figure it out for himself.

But since the moment Emma'd hopped into her car and driven away, he hadn't been able to think of anything else but her. And that was just way too weird.

"I saw her the other night," he said, and instantly a vivid image of Emma in that short, tight skirt leaped into his mind and hovered there to torment him.

"So?" Aidan moved in closer, taking the beer from Brian's hand and draining it.

"Hey!" Brian complained.

"Get another one, geez," Aidan sniped.

Sunshine poured down on the concrete driveway and bounced off the cement surface to surround the brothers in steamy summer heat. Hardly a breath moved through the trees and there wasn't a cloud in sight. But they'd made plans to play basketball today and come hell or dehydration, they were going to play.

Brian snapped the top on another beer and held it far away from Aidan's reach. Taking a drink, he glanced from Connor to Liam and winked. "Hey, looks like you've got another brother about to topple."

Connor straightened up and scowled at him. "No way. I can make it. Unlike *some* people."

Brian just laughed. "Hey, I don't get the money, but I *do* get laid. *Often*."

"Bastard," Aidan muttered, then added, "can't understand why a woman as great as Tina would put up with you."

"She wanted the best," Brian assured him.

"Yeah, yeah." Aidan threw the ball at him, Brian caught it and sent it toward the hoop.

As they moved off, Liam stepped up to Connor and slapped him on the back. "So, anything you'd like to share with your friendly neighborhood brother slash priest?"

Connor shook his head. "You're in no position to give advice on women, Liam. I may be out of the game for two more months, but you're in it for life."

Liam shrugged, reached down into the open cooler beside him and pulled out two cans of beer. Tossing one to Connor, he opened one for himself and said, "I wasn't born into the priesthood, you know."

"Yeah, I remember."

"So? Feel like talking?"

"No." Connor took a long gulp of the beer and felt the icy froth race down his throat and send a welcome chill throughout his body. But it wouldn't help for long, he knew. Ever since seeing Emma at the Off Duty, he'd been hot and hadn't been able to cool off. Thoughts of her plagued him. Memories of the way she moved, the way she smiled, the way she smelled, were becoming a part of him.

Which was exactly why he'd stayed away from her garage the past couple of days. He needed space. Time. He needed to figure out just what the hell had happened to him the other night. And until he did, it wasn't safe for him to be around Emma.

Going into his second month of forced celibacy, Connor was balancing precariously on a razor's edge of control. One little push either way, and he was a goner.

And the way Emma had looked the other night, she was just the one to give him that push.

"That's it?" Liam asked. "Just *no?*"

"Liam, the day I need a priest's advice on women, is the day you can shave my head and send me to Okinawa."

"You're a Marine, moron," Liam reminded him, setting down his beer and moving back to the top of the basketball court, where Aidan and Brian were dueling it out. "Your head's already shaved and you've *been* to Okinawa."

Connor scowled at him.

Hell, maybe he *did* need advice from a priest.

# Five

"**H**e hasn't been back, Mary Alice." Emma leaned back in the office chair that had once belonged to her father and was now all hers.

"You expected him to come running right over?"

"Well, *yeah*." She twirled the coiled telephone cord around her index finger so tightly her skin turned bluish purple. Quickly she unwound it again. "If you could have seen him drooling all over me, you would have thought so, too."

"Uh-huh," Mary Alice said, "and what were you doing while he was drooling?"

"You mean besides falling out of my top?"

"Yeah. Were you drooling back?"

"A little maybe." Okay, *a lot*. But she couldn't

very well admit that to Mary Alice, could she? Not when her friend had warned her going in that this was a bad idea? Oh, maybe it *had* been a bad idea.

For two days now Emma'd been doing little else but think about Connor. Which was weird. He'd been a part of her life for two years, but until this week, she'd never once imagined him naked in bed with her. And, oh, boy, her imagination was *really* good.

"I knew it," the voice on the phone said, disgusted. "I knew you'd be setting yourself up again. Honestly, Em…"

"This is different," Emma protested, not sure if she was trying to reassure her friend or herself. Memories of three years ago and a broken engagement darted through her mind and were just as quickly extinguished. "I'm not looking for forever," she said. "Just a little right now."

"Uh-huh."

Emma scowled at the phone. "You don't have to sound so unconvinced."

"Please, Em. You are *so* not the one-night-stand kind of woman."

She stiffened. "I could be."

"Yeah, and I could be a runway model, if not for the extra twenty pounds."

"Funny."

"I'm not trying to be funny," Mary Alice said. "I'm *trying* to make you come to your senses before you get in so deep with this guy that your heart gets broken again."

"Wow. First Father Liam warns me about the dangers of seduction turning into love and now you." Emma blew out a breath. "My heart is perfectly safe. It's my hormones that are getting the work out."

Well, that set Mary Alice off. A floodgate of warnings poured from her, and she barely paused for breath.

While she listened to her friend's worries pouring through the receiver, Emma glanced around the tiny Jacobsen "empire."

The office was filled with potted plants, and flowering vines fell from baskets hanging in the corners of the room. The wide glass windows gleamed in the sunlight and gave Emma a bird's-eye view of the flower beds lining the front of the shop. Zinnias and petunias added color and scent to the shop and welcomed customers with unexpected beauty.

Her father had started the business more than thirty years ago and had never really concerned himself with making the place "pretty." He'd built a reputation based on honesty and fair prices and when he passed away five years before, he'd left that business in Emma's capable hands.

She knew her way around an engine—hard to grow up the only child of a mechanic and *not* learn— but as she'd helped the business grow, Emma had found herself spending more time lately on paperwork than on actual engines. Though there was still nothing she loved better than restoring classic cars.

The two mechanics she had working for her were

good at their jobs and didn't have a problem taking orders from a woman—especially one who could do a tune-up in less than thirty minutes.

"Hello? Earth to Emma."

"Huh? What?" Emma shook her head, sighed deeply and said, "Sorry. Zoned out there for a minute."

"I'm giving you all this great advice and you're not listening?"

"I didn't say that. I heard you. I just think you're going a little overboard."

"No such thing. You're not experienced enough with guys to know how to protect yourself."

"Gee, *Mom,* thanks."

"You *did* call me to talk about this, remember?"

"Yeah," she paused and pushed a long strand of blond hair behind her ear. She'd given in to a weak moment and called her best friend in the world because Emma was getting a little nervous. This wasn't working out quite the way she'd planned it. She was supposed to be driving Connor insane with desire— not herself. "I remember."

"So, talk to me."

"I already told you about the other night at the bar."

"Yeah," Mary Alice said with a sigh. "Wish I could have seen you balancing on those heels while playing pool."

"Hey, I'm better at it than I used to be." She grinned, though, remembering how many times she'd fallen on her behind when Mary Alice had coached her through actually *walking* in high heels. That had only been four years ago. When she'd first decided to remake herself in the hopes of falling in love. Back before she realized that love only really mattered if the guy was in love with the *real* Emma.

"God, I should hope so," she chuckled, then continued, "so you said Connor was all droolly, right?"

"Like a starving man looking at a steak."

"This is a good thing."

"Yes, but I haven't seen him since." Damn it. Emma'd thought for sure that Connor would come by the garage the day after their pool match. The way he'd stared at her breasts and her legs, she'd have bet money on him being completely hooked.

She would have lost.

"Figure he's avoiding you on purpose?"

"Seems like that's the case."

"Then you must have worried him."

Emma smiled, dropped her feet from the desk and sat up. "Hey…I hadn't really thought about it like that."

"If he doesn't trust himself around you, I'd say you're close to getting him to lose the bet."

"Good point." She'd been so busy being annoyed that Connor was keeping his distance, Emma'd never really asked herself *why* he was suddenly so determined to avoid her. Maybe he wasn't thinking of her as a pal anymore, and that had him worried. Maybe her too-tight skirt and too-small shirt had done the deed after all.

But then why didn't he come over for another look, damn it?

She stood up and walked around the edge of the desk, stretching the coiled phone cord as far as it would go. Outside, the summer sun blasted down on the city streets, heat shimmering in the air, giving Baywater the wavering look of a mirage. On the main street traffic bumped along, and as she watched, a black SUV made the turn into the garage's driveway.

A chill swept instantly down her spine, and Emma tried to tell herself it was just the icy breeze from the air conditioner affecting her. But she knew better.

She licked suddenly dry lips. "He's here."

"What?"

"Connor," Emma said, her fingers tightening on the receiver. She watched him step out of his car and wince as the heat slapped at him. Oh, he looked way too good. Despite the summer heat, he wore faded jeans that clung to his long legs. His white T-shirt strained across his broad chest, and his jaw was tight and set as he stuffed his keys into his pocket and headed for the office—and her.

A jolt of pure anticipation lit up her insides and made her mouth water.

"What's he look like?" Mary Alice demanded.

"Dessert," Emma groaned. "Gotta go." She hung up while her friend was still talking, then eased one hip against the corner of her desk and tried to look nonchalant. Not at all easy when your stomach is spinning and your heartbeat is crashing in your ears.

Emma couldn't take her gaze off him, and she wondered just when this little game she'd started had turned on her. He was the one who was supposed to be going all gooey-eyed, not *her*. But here she stood, watching his long legs move across the parking lot and wishing he'd turn around so she could get a glimpse of his very nice behind.

Her stomach took another nosedive, and she slapped one hand against it as he opened the door and stepped inside. Instantly her small office felt darn near claustrophobic.

Connor ground his back teeth together as he looked at her. Big mistake coming here. After leaving his brothers, he'd gone home to take a shower, but hadn't been able to sit still. Thoughts of Emma had plagued him as they had been for the past two days, and he'd finally decided there was only one thing to do about it.

If he hoped to keep his friendship with her, then he needed to stay the hell away from her for the duration of this stupid bet.

He wasn't about to risk his nice, easy relationship with Emma just because he was so damn horny he could hardly see straight. Emma was his *friend*. The bet was the only reason he was acting like a moron around her now. And damn it, he wouldn't give in to it. He was no teenager stuck on the first girl to smile at him.

He was a Marine.

He was tough.

He was hard.

And getting harder by the second.

His gaze swept over her quickly, thoroughly. She was wearing a pair of pale-green coverall shorts that displayed miles of smooth, tanned leg. And under the bibbed coverall, was a dark-pink tank top edged with lace. Her blond hair was pulled into a high ponytail and then braided into a thick rope that lay across her right shoulder. And his fingers itched to touch it. He wanted to undo the tight braid and rake his hands through the softness.

*Whoa.*

He stiffened slightly, instinctively shifting into a *braced for battle* position. Feet wide apart, arms crossed over his chest. Ordering himself to stand down, he knew, more than ever, that he'd done the right thing in coming here. He had to explain to her that he wouldn't be seeing her for the next couple of months. Had to tell her—what?

That he didn't trust himself around her?

That he all of a sudden was spending way too much time thinking about her trim little body?

That he wanted to sink his teeth into her shoulders and then lick his way down the length of her?

Oh, yeah. That'd be real smart.

"Emma, we have to talk." The words came out a little harder than he'd planned, but then, his jaw was clenched so tight every word was an effort of will.

"Really?" She smiled and edged off the corner of the desk.

Her sandals were white with little daisies on the top strap. Her toenails were painted the same dark shade of pink as her tank top, and she wore a gold toe ring that winked and sparkled in the sunlight. Damn it. Mechanics don't wear jewelry on their feet.

He frowned. "Since when do you wear a toe ring?"

She looked down, then up at him. "Since three years ago."

"Oh." He scraped one hand across his face. Something else he'd never noticed. Or if he had, it had been ignored, because Emma was his friend. His buddy. But that was then, and this was now. "Look, Emma, about the other night—"

"What about it?" She moved a little closer and he got a whiff of her perfume.

The soft, haunting scent reached for his throat and squeezed. This was risky. Being this close to her. He should have called her. Should have kept his distance. But he hadn't wanted to, and at least he could admit that much to himself.

Hell, he couldn't figure out why this was happening to him at all. He'd never spent much time fantasizing about one particular woman. To Connor, women were like candy. You never wanted to stick with one too long, because you'd just get tired of it. He was a big believer in the "variety is the spice of life" theory on romance.

But since seeing Emma at the bar the other night, she'd been right up at the forefront of his mind. He hadn't been able to shake her. Hell, he hadn't been able to make himself *try*.

"You surprised me," he said.

She stepped closer, and her scent moved in for the

kill. Damn it, she was wrapped around him now and he couldn't breathe without taking a piece of her inside him.

"Yeah, you said that already."

"Right." He had said it. Outside in the parking lot. When he'd tried to convince her *and* himself that he'd been surprised by her pool-playing abilities. He frowned, shook his head and looked down at her. Her summer-sky eyes were wide and incredibly blue. A man could lose himself just staring into those depths. And he didn't want to be lost.

"Look," he blurted, taking a hasty step back, hopefully out of range of her force field. "You want to go get some lunch or something?"

Her blond eyebrows lifted high on her forehead. "You're asking me to lunch?"

"Something wrong with that?" he demanded, as he silently cursed himself. For God's sake, you don't get over a woman by asking her out to eat. "Can't two friends share a meal together without making a big deal out of it?"

Her lips twitched, then her mouth slowly curved and he felt a tug of reaction deep inside him.

"Who's making a big deal about anything?"

"Nobody," he said, nodding as if trying to convince himself. "Not a big deal. Just lunch." He frowned. "So? You interested?"

"Sure. Just let me tell the guys I'm leaving."

She walked through the connecting door to the garage bay and God help him, Connor watched her go.

Man. Short coveralls had never looked so good. There was nothing "friendly" in the way his gaze locked onto her—and he knew he was digging himself an even deeper hole.

Delilah's Diner was relaxed and casual.

Tourists and locals mingled together and the low hum of activity echoed throughout the place. Booths lined one wall by the window overlooking Pine Avenue. A dozen or more round tables were dotted around the rest of the room, with a long lunch counter sweeping around the back. Waitresses moved through the crowd with dazzling speed and the "order ready" bell rang out with regularity.

Emma leaned back against the white Naugahyde booth seat and folded her arms on the scrubbed red vinyl tabletop. Connor hadn't spoken to her at all since leaving the shop, and now he looked as if he'd rather be anywhere but here.

How was a girl supposed to take that?

While they waited for their order, she reached for her glass of water and took a long sip before asking, "So are you going to be silent all through lunch?"

"Huh?"

"You said you wanted to talk, but you haven't even opened your mouth since we left the garage."

"Miss the sound of my voice?"

He grinned, and the quick smile jolted something deep inside her. Emma took a long drink of water in an attempt to drown it.

"What's going on, Connor?"

"Nothing, it's just that—"

Their waitress chose just that moment to arrive with their meals. She slid Emma's chef salad across the table then carefully placed Connor's hamburger and fries directly in front of him. Emma rolled her eyes and watched, half amused, half irritated as the woman did everything but coo and stroke Connor's chest.

"Thanks," he said, smiling up at the redhead.

"You bet," the woman said on a sigh, barely sparing a glance for Emma. "If there's anything else you need—" she paused meaningfully "—anything at all, you just call me. I'm Rebecca."

"Thanks, Rebecca," Emma spoke up, startling the waitress out of her flirtatious mood. "We'll call if we need you."

The woman flashed her a frown, then shot Connor another smile before reluctantly wandering off.

"Amazing," Emma said, shaking her head in disgust.

"What?"

"You didn't notice?"

He picked up his hamburger and took a bite. Shrugging, he chewed and repeated, "Notice what?"

"Unbelievable. But then why would you?" Emma asked, not really expecting an answer. "You've probably affected women like that your whole life."

"What the hell are you talking about?"

"The redheaded waitress?" Emma coaxed. "The one who wants to have your child—here on the table?"

He laughed and picked up a French fry. "Don't you think you're exaggerating a little?"

She stabbed a forkful of lettuce and chicken and really considered stabbing him in the hand just for the heck of it. No wonder he'd never paid attention to her. He had women crawling all over him all the time. The man was a babe magnet. Any female between the ages of fifteen and fifty would turn for another look at him. "No, I'm not."

Connor shrugged. "She probably thinks I'm Aidan. He eats in here a lot."

She just stared at him. She'd never had any trouble at all telling the triplets apart. Sure, they were identical, but there was a little something different about each of them that made all the difference. With Connor, it was the way the right corner of his mouth lifted when he didn't really want to smile but couldn't help himself.

"What was it like?" she asked. "Growing up with two other people who look just like you?"

His mouth curved, just the way she liked it.

"Fun. We had a great time, the three of us. And Liam, too, before he went into the seminary." He paused and looked at her. "I can't imagine growing up like you did. An only child."

She lifted one shoulder and took another bite of her salad. "It was okay. My dad and I got along fine, just the two of us."

"Yeah, I bet you did. But you didn't have somebody to trade places with at exam time."

"You didn't."

"Sure we did." Connor laughed and his eyes flashed with memories. "Aidan's the brain. So come chemistry finals—he took all of our tests."

Emma laughed and shook her head. "I can't believe you got away with that."

"We did. For the first two years of high school. After that the teacher wised up. Noticed that all three of us answered every question the same way."

"What happened when you got caught?"

He winced, then winked at her. "Let's just say our mother is more than a match for her sons. None of us saw the outside world for a solid month."

"Even Liam?" Emma reached for her ice tea. "He was innocent."

"Yeah, but he was the oldest. Mom figured he should have kept us out of trouble."

While Connor talked about his brothers, Emma watched him and tried to remember that she wasn't supposed to be getting more deeply involved in his life. This was just a seduction. Pure and simple. A plot to get him to lose a bet and be sorry he'd ever dismissed her.

But he smiled and she forgot about her plan. He laughed and she just enjoyed the loud, rolling sound of it pouring over her. Beneath the table, his foot brushed her leg, and she felt the punch of electrical awareness dance up her calf, past her thigh to simmer in a spot that was already too hot for comfort.

He felt it, too; she sensed it.

His gaze locked with hers across the table, and the humor in his eyes faded slowly away to be replaced by a slow burn of hunger that scorched her, even at a distance. "What're we doing, Emma?"

"Having lunch?" she asked, swallowing hard and trying to steady her breathing.

"What else?"

"Is there something else, Connor?"

"I didn't want there to be, but it's damn hard to ignore."

A spurt of disappointment shot through her but didn't do a thing toward cooling the fires within. "Well, that was flattering."

"Emma, we're friends." He leaned across the table and took her hand in his. His thumb scraped her palm until the tingles of sensation speared through her.

She blew out a breath, but didn't let go of his hand. She liked the feel of his fingers entwined with hers. Liked the heat she found pulsing in him and the flames awakening in herself. "And friends don't see each other naked?"

"Not usually," he admitted, through gritted teeth.

She nodded slowly and, just as slowly, reluctantly, pulled her hand free of his. "Then we'll just have to stop being friends, won't we, Connor?"

# Six

*Stop being friends?*

Emma's words hit Connor like a fist to the gut. "That's exactly what I'm trying to avoid," he muttered, his hand tingling with emptiness now that she'd let go of him. He rubbed the tips of his fingers together, as if he could still feel the silky slide of her skin on his. Damn it. He didn't have so many close friends that he was willing to lose one. Especially *this* one. He and Emma always had a good time together. They could talk about anything. He could laugh with her. Tell her what he was thinking.

When the new recruits in his charge were starting to drive him up the wall with frustration, Connor knew he could go to Emma's and forget about the world for a while. When his brothers made him nuts, she laughed with him about it. When the rest of the world looked less than warm and welcoming, Emma's smile set it right.

And he wasn't ready or willing to give that up.

"You can't always get what you want," she said with a little shrug that nudged the strap of her coveralls down her left shoulder.

He scowled at her. What was *that* supposed to mean? Did she *want* to end their friendship and try something different? Or was she trying to tell him that she wasn't interested in sex with him?

Why couldn't women be as clear as men?

"Don't start quoting song lyrics at me."

"A little touchy, aren't we?" she asked.

"Not touchy, just surprised you're so damn willing to toss our friendship for a quick roll in the hay."

"I didn't say *that,* either."

He actually *felt* his scowl deepen. "Then just what the hell are you saying?"

"Not much," she said, and her voice was cool, amused, even. "Just that if you want to go to bed, we'll stop being friends. If you don't, we won't."

"Oh, so it's all up to me?" He didn't believe that for a damn minute. There wasn't a woman alive who wasn't completely at the wheel of any relationship. And all men knew it. They just pretended otherwise to hang on to their pride.

Which was *precisely* why he'd always avoided commitment like the plague. Once a woman got a good hold on you, things changed. Your life wasn't your own anymore. You were going to chick movies regularly and worrying about putting coasters under your bottle of beer.

Not worth the effort. Leave the married life for people like Brian. For Connor, it was love 'em and leave 'em—quick.

She shook her head, and he watched that thick, honey-gold braid swing from side to side like a pendulum. "Up entirely to you? Not a chance. Look, you just said yourself you didn't *want* there to be anything else between us."

"Yeah, but—" Not fair to use a man's own words against him.

"So, there's no problem, right?"

He scraped one hand over his face. Something was wrong. Somewhere or other he'd lost the thread of this conversation, and he wasn't sure any more which side he should be defending. Damn it, a man needed a battle plan to deal with a woman. Any woman.

Especially, it seemed, *this* woman.

Emma grinned, tilted her head to one side to stare at him, and her thick, blond braid swung over her right shoulder. He wanted to reach across the table, undo the rubber band at the end of it and comb her hair free, burying his fingers in it.

"Do I make you nervous, Connor?"

"No." The answer came sharp and swift, and he had to wonder if he was trying to convince Emma or himself. Dismissing the idea entirely, he picked up his hamburger, took a bite and chewed like a man on a mission. However he'd lost control of this conversation, he could still get it back.

After he swallowed, he said, "I'm not *nervous*."

"Then what's the problem?"

*Problem?* Where to start? How about sitting across from his friend in a lunch diner and knowing he'd need about twenty minutes before he could stand up and walk out of there without embarrassing himself? How about the fact that he could smell her perfume—something a little different today, flowers and...lemons, but just as intoxicating.

He couldn't tell her any of that. Just as he couldn't tell her that he'd been lying awake at nights imagining her *naked*. That would damage the very friendship he was fighting so hard not to lose.

This was all his brothers' faults. Every last one of 'em. Brian being so happily married now—and delighting in telling Connor and Aidan about all the sex he was currently enjoying. Aidan being so determined to being the last man standing. And even Liam, standing on the sidelines, laughing at all of them as they tried to do for three months what he'd committed to for a lifetime.

He never should have made the stupid bet.

It'd been a pain in the butt from the get go.

And it was only getting worse.

"Damn it, Em," he muttered thickly, fighting past the knot of need lodged in his throat, "it's the bet. You know that's what's behind all of this."

"Uh-huh."

He frowned at her less-than-convinced reply. When she took another bite of salad, then delicately licked a drop of dressing off her bottom lip, every cell in Connor's body lit up like a fireworks show. Inwardly groaning, he squashed the lightninglike flash of need bursting to life inside him.

"Look," he said, leaning toward her and lowering his voice to be sure none of the other diners could overhear, "we both know this bet is making me nuts. We both know that we're *friends*, nothing more."

She nodded and smiled. "You bet."

He inhaled sharply, deeply. His stomach knotted and he glanced down at his hamburger in sudden distaste. He couldn't force a bite down his tight throat now if someone had a gun to his head. Pushing the plate aside, he leaned both forearms on the table and held her gaze with his own. "I *like* you, Emma."

"Thanks, Connor," she said, daintily picking a piece of chicken out of her salad and popping it into her mouth. "I like you, too."

"Exactly!" He slapped one hand against the tabletop with enough force to make the iced tea glasses jump and shudder.

Several people turned to look at him, and Emma laughed. He didn't care.

"That's my point." He glanced around warily, then lowered his voice again. He felt like a secret agent in a bad movie. "We *like* each other too much to climb into bed together."

"Okay."

He sat back, stunned. *"Okay?"*

She shrugged again and this time the tiny spaghetti strap of her little tank top slid off her shoulder to join the strap of her coveralls. Connor gritted his teeth.

"Sure," she was saying, and he blinked away the haze of pure, one-hundred-proof lust clouding his mind so he could listen. "I mean it's no biggie to me. If you'd rather not, then fine."

"Just like that."

She smiled. "Did you expect me to throw myself across the table and plead with you to *take me now, big boy?*"

Maybe a little, he admitted silently. He'd thought sure she was feeling what he was feeling. That she'd wanted him as much as he had her. But apparently not. And why didn't that make him feel better?

"Sorry to disappoint you, Connor," she said, and idly lifted both straps off her upper arm to slide them into place. "But I'll survive if we don't hit the sheets together."

"I know that," he said, and wondered how in the hell this had all turned around. When had he set himself up to be turned down? When had *she* become the one to say no?

"Good." She took another bite of her salad and if she hadn't just a second ago told him she wasn't disappointed by the thought of not going to bed with him—Connor would have thought she was licking her lip deliberately. She did it slowly—tantalizingly slowly—and his body, still at DefCon 1 lit up like a demilitarized zone during a night landing.

She picked up her iced tea, took a long drink, and Connor's gaze fixed on the line of her throat. His vision blurred.

Then she set her glass down, glanced at her watch and said, "Oops! Gotta run."

"Now? You're leaving now?"

"I really have to," she explained, gathering up her brown leather purse and slinging it over her left shoulder. "But you go ahead and stay. The shop's only a block away. I'll walk it."

When he didn't say anything, she stopped scooting toward the edge of the booth. "Connor? Was there something else you wanted to talk about?"

"No," he grumbled. "Nothing at all."

"Okay, good." She leaned toward him and smiled. "I've got a bad carburetor coming into the shop in twenty minutes, so I have to be there."

"Right." He grabbed his own iced tea glass and cradled it between his palms, letting the cold seep into his skin, his bones.

She stood up and flashed him another smile as he looked up at her. Then she dropped one hand onto his shoulder and he swore he could feel the warmth of her skin right through the fabric of his shirt.

"I'll see you later, okay? And thanks for lunch."

"Right. Later." He nodded and swallowed hard.

She walked away and he couldn't help himself. He turned on the booth seat to watch her go and groaned as his gaze locked onto the curve of her behind. Grumbling under his breath, he turned back around and squirmed uncomfortably on the bench seat.

Rebecca, the friendly waitress, hustled right over and asked, "Can I get you anything else?"

He didn't even meet her eyes this time. Instead he drained his iced tea, then handed her the empty glass. He wasn't going anywhere until his body cooled down. Shouldn't take more than an hour—and since he couldn't very well take a cold shower, he'd have to settle for cold drinks. And maybe he should just pour the next one in his lap where it would do the most good.

"Bring me another one of these, would you? And make it a large."

She frowned, but he didn't notice.

Or care.

Later that evening Connor drove from his apartment to the base. Sick of his own company, he'd decided to check in with his assistant drill sergeant. Now, watching the young troops trying to settle into life as Marines, he at least had something else to think about besides himself.

And they *were* young.

Most of them still in their teens, they were driven to the recruit depot at Parris Island at night. Brought across the long road winding into the base past swamp water and marsh grasses in the dark. Deliberately. Not to disorient, but to have them connect to *this* world almost instantly. To remind them that they and their fellow recruits were now a team. A family. That they'd become a part of something much bigger than they'd ever known before, and that the life they left behind had no place here.

Standing in the corner of the barracks, Connor watched DI Jeff McDonald striding up and down the aisle separating two long rows of bunks. Each new recruit stood in front of their beds, heads newly shaved, narrow shoulders thrown back and chins jutted out.

"Boy," McDonald shouted, stopping in front of a tall, thin kid, "did I just see you *smile?*"

"Sir! No, sir!"

Connor smothered a grin and watched as McDonald feigned disgust.

"You think you're going to a party, recruit?"

"Sir! No, sir!"

McDonald leaned in closer, his nose just a hair's breadth from the kid's. He pointed to the chevrons on his sleeve. "Then you better stop smiling recruit, or I'm gonna think you think I'm funny lookin.'"

The kid looked horrified by the idea.

"Do you think I'm funny lookin,' recruit?"

"Sir! No, sir!"

Connor watched from the shadows and silently approved. McDonald was good at his job. He'd intimidate the recruits, teach them what they needed to know to survive, and in the end he'd have their respect. And he would have turned out a new company of Marines.

Smiling, Connor told himself the kid would learn. They all would. Or they wouldn't make the grade. But most of them would. They were here because they wanted something more and, generally, were willing to work for it.

Connor shook his head, shoved his hands into his pockets and slipped out the side door. The summer night was warm, the air felt thick with the scent of the South and the humidity that was such a part of life here.

He stopped and tilted his head back to stare up at the black, star-studded sky. Things were running as they should be here. He wasn't needed. McDonald didn't have time to talk, and he wasn't in the mood to hunt down any of his other friends.

He still had days to go on his leave time. Hell, he should be *itching* to get into town. To grab a beer. Play some pool at the Off Duty.

Connor winced. He had the distinct feeling he'd never again be able to stroll into that bar without his brain replaying the image of Emma bent over the pool table, taking a shot. He scrubbed both hands over his face and shook himself like a big dog climbing out of a lake.

They'd settled *nothing* at lunch.

If anything, he'd only walked away more confused than he had been before.

So the only way to get this clear in his mind was

to go and see Emma. Talk to her. Figure out what the hell it was that was driving him and then find a way to end it.

And if a small, rational voice in the back of his mind was warning him to steer clear of Emma Jacobsen—he wasn't listening.

Emma sat on her back porch, staring up at the sky.

Star Jasmine flavored the warm, moist air and stirred in the gentle breeze that swept through the yard, then disappeared again. Sighing, she leaned against a porch post and stretched her legs out, down the steps leading to the grassy yard. She reached for the frosty margarita sitting beside her and lifted it for a sip.

Ordinarily she didn't drink much.

But after her lunch with Connor, and a long, dreary day of rebuilding a carburetor and then the depressing conversation with Mrs. Harrison, she'd felt she'd earned a drink or two.

Mrs. Florence Harrison, a widow who lived just outside of town had been disappointing Emma for two years now. All because of a '58 Corvette currently rusting in Mrs. Harrison's barn. The car had once belonged to the woman's son, now dead forty years. Emma had lusted after the 'Vette ever since the moment she'd first seen it. She longed to bring it into the garage and restore it to its full glory.

But Mrs. Harrison flatly refused to part with her late son's "baby."

"Ah, well," Emma said, and took a long, deep

drink of the frothy concoction in her glass. She let the icy stream wash down her throat and send chills to every corner of her body. "What's one more *no* in the grand scheme of things, anyway?"

Connor didn't want her enough to lose the bet, and Mrs. Harrison was clutching that Corvette to her bosom like a long-lost child.

Pushing off the top step, Emma stood up and walked down the stairs and across the lawn. The damp grass felt cool and lush beneath her bare feet as she wandered aimlessly through the shadows. From down the street, she heard snatches of sound, letting her know her neighbors were also enjoying the cool relief of the summer night. Children laughed, dogs barked and the faint sound of a radio playing caught the air and hung on it.

When the wind kicked up suddenly, it swept through her hair, lifting it off her neck into a wild, brief dance. At the side of the house, the wind chimes tinkled merrily, and she smiled at the sound, in spite of everything.

"What're you thinking?"

The deep, familiar voice came from somewhere close beside her, and Emma's stomach jumped as she turned to face Connor. "You scared me," she said, though that wasn't strictly true.

Startled, yes. But scared? Nope. Much closer to a rush of hunger than a rush of fear. Funny how she'd never noticed before now just what kind of effect his voice had on her. Just when exactly had *that* started happening?

"Sorry. Didn't mean to sneak up on you," he said, and took a step closer. "But you looked like you were thinking serious thoughts—then you smiled. Intrigued me."

Still in the USMC T-shirt and jeans he'd been wearing earlier, Connor looked good enough to fuel dozens of dreams. At the thought she clutched her margarita glass a little tighter and took a sip, even as she acknowledged that it was false courage. "I, um, just liked the sound of the wind chimes."

As if awaiting a cue, the wind breathed past them again, and the chimes sounded out like fairy bells.

"Pretty," he said.

"Yeah, they are."

"Not them," he said. *"You."*

Whoa.

Head rush.

It wasn't the margarita. She hadn't had enough of that to matter. It was Connor. Plain and simple. In the moonlit darkness, he looked impossibly handsome. His strong jaw worked as though his teeth were clenched. His eyes were as dark as sapphires, and the reflection of stars danced in them. His mouth was tightened into a grim slash that made him look as though he regretted saying those words.

Well, too bad if he did.

He *had* said them and there was no going back now.

"Thank you."

"Emma…"

"Connor," she interrupted him neatly and took another sip of her drink to stall for a precious second or two. "If you're here to tell me again what a great pal I am and how you don't want to lose me—" she stopped and took a breath. "You don't have to bother. I get it. Understood. Go. Be happy. Fly free."

He glanced around the empty yard, and she knew he wasn't noticing the lushly crowded flower beds or the sweet smelling jasmine vines clinging to the fence wrapping around her property. He was waiting, thinking, maybe having as difficult a time as she was with whatever it was that lay between them.

And for one brief moment Emma wondered if she'd done the right thing in setting this ball in motion. But there was no turning back. No avoiding whatever was coming.

Finally he looked at her and she read a decision in his eyes. She lifted her chin and braced herself for whatever was coming next.

"This isn't about our friendship, Em," he said softly. "This is about what's making me crazy."

"And what's that?" Oh, man. She held her breath and felt the sense of waiting all through her body.

"If I don't kiss you in the next ten seconds, I think I'm gonna lose what's left of my mind."

All of the air left her body and fire replaced it. She felt tongues of flame working their way through her insides. Her body went hot and ready and eager. Her mind clicked off and her emotions charged to the surface. But her voice was steady as she smiled up at him. "Time's awastin' then."

He grabbed her.

She dropped the acrylic margarita glass to the ground, spilling the icy drink across the grass.

He pulled her hard against him, stared deeply into her eyes for one heart-stoppingly long moment.

And then he kissed her.

# Seven

Connor hung on to Emma as if it meant his life.

And in that moment maybe it did.

For the past several days, she'd filled his mind. Every thought, every dream was stamped with her image.

She fit against him as if she was the missing piece to his puzzle. And though one corner of his brain clanged out a warning bell, he refused to listen.

His arms wrapped around her, pulling her close, closer. His hands swept up and down her back, aligning her body with his, until he felt every inch of her pressed to him tightly enough that he felt her heartbeat fluttering wildly. His mouth took hers, his tongue tangling with hers in an erotic dance that fired his system with a need unlike anything he'd ever known before.

She sighed into his mouth, and he swallowed her breath, taking it inside and holding it. Her arms linked at the back of his neck, and she pressed herself even more fully against him.

He felt the pressure of her pebbled nipples pressing into his chest, branding his skin with heat that seared him right down to his soul. Connor groaned, and his arms tightened around her, lifting her feet clean off the ground.

Again and again their tongues tangled in a dance as old as time and as new as sunrise. She tasted of her icy drink and tantalizing secrets. He couldn't get enough of her.

Somewhere in the back of his mind, a voice shouted, *This is Emma.* His pal.

His buddy.

And right now the only thing in his life he desperately wanted.

Tearing his mouth from hers, he gasped for air like a wild man. Blindly, Connor stared down at her and saw her familiar features through a bristling red haze of passion. Her mouth was swollen from his kiss. Her summer-blue eyes were glazed with the same desire blasting through him. Her breath labored in and out of her lungs, and he wondered if her heart was thundering in her chest—as his was.

"Wow." She blinked up at him and smiled with all the wonder of a kid at Christmas, unwrapping a gift she hadn't even been aware of wanting.

Connor knew just how she felt. "Yeah," he said, "I think that just about covers it."

"Who would have guessed?"

He set her back onto her feet and released his viselike hold on her. Still, though, he was reluctant to break all contact. He lifted one hand and stroked her cheek with his fingertips. Her skin was as warm as sunlight and as soft as velvet.

Emma turned her face into his touch and closed her eyes as he caressed her face. She sighed a little, opened her eyes again and said, "Why *did* you come here tonight, Connor?"

*Good question.* He wasn't entirely sure he had an answer for her. Shaking his head, he said simply, "I don't really know. I just drove here. Didn't actually stop and think about it. Didn't plan it. Just followed my instincts and they led me here."

"Instincts, huh?"

He nodded and shoved one hand along the side of his head. Hard to admit, even to himself, that it was pure gut reflex that had brought him to Emma's door. But there it was. As a Marine, he'd learned long ago to trust the impulses that drove him. He didn't question, didn't doubt. He just *did.* That confidence in his own subconscious had saved his butt more than once.

And tonight those instincts had brought him here. To Emma.

"What are they telling you to do now?"

If he told her that, she'd probably run for the hills. Because it was taking all of his self-control to keep from tearing her clothes off and tossing her onto the cool, damp grass. He wanted her naked. He wanted her beneath him. Over him. Astride him. He wanted her in every possible way, and as they stood there in the starlit shadows, that want continued to pulse and grow. "You don't wanna know."

She stepped up close, close enough that he could feel the heat of her body radiating out around her. "Yes, I do."

Her scent lifted into the air and filled his mind. The taste of her still lingered on his tongue. His blood raced, his body tightened until the pain of waiting was almost as fierce as the desire gnawing at him.

He hadn't meant to start this. To light a match to the stick of dynamite lying between them. But now that the first, most difficult, step had been taken, now that the lit fuse was lying there sparking and sizzling, there was no going back. Though his brain shouted at him to think about what he was doing, what he was thinking, his body wasn't listening.

His mouth hungered for another taste. His hands burned to touch her, to sweep along her skin, define every inch of the compact, curvy body that had been plaguing him.

"If you don't want this to happen," he managed to grind out, "say so now."

She was breathing as heavily as he was. Even in the pearly moonlight, he saw the flush on her cheeks and the glitter in her eyes. And he prayed—desperately—that when she made her decision it would be one he could live with. One that wouldn't haunt them both. Even as he thought it, though, he realized that the hell of it was, no matter what she said, they would be haunted.

Because after *this* night, nothing between them would ever be the same—whatever happened.

"If I didn't want this," she pointed out, "you would have known about it when you kissed me."

"Be sure," he said, and wasn't entirely sure himself why he was giving her this out. Why he was practically daring her to call a halt to this. Because if she did say no—it was going to kill him.

"I'm sure, Connor. Are you?"

"Decision made, babe." He grabbed her again, filling his hands with the thin fabric of her tank top. He pulled her close again and dipped his head to take her mouth with his. To drown in the taste of her. She sighed into him, and Connor's blood raced through his veins, thick and hot. He groaned, broke the kiss and stared down at her for a long second, before picking her up and tossing her over his shoulder.

"Hey!" She braced her palms against his lower back, pushed herself up and shouted, "What the hell are you doing?"

"I'm through wasting time, Em." He slapped his palm against her butt, and when she yelped, he grinned.

"What are you, a caveman?"

"Caveman, Marine…you tell me."

"I will if you'll put me down."

"Not a chance." He marched across the moonlit backyard, took the five steps to the back porch at a dead run, then yanked open the screen door and stepped into her kitchen.

He paid no attention to the homey room with its glass-fronted cabinets. He glanced at the blender full of margaritas, then kept walking, out of the kitchen to the bottom of the stairs. He'd been to her house before. He knew his way around the ground floor—but he'd never been upstairs. Never been into her bedroom. Never even considered it until tonight. But that was then—this was now.

"Damn it, Connor," she said, slamming her fist against his back, "I mean it. Put me down."

"As soon as I see a bed. Trust me. I'll put you down. Where'm I headed?"

She sighed, then laughed, and the magic of it floated in the air like soap bubbles on a summer wind. "Upstairs, you Neanderthal. First door on the left."

"Got it." He took the stairs two at a time, his long legs making short work of the trip. Emma's slight yet curvy body hooked over his shoulder didn't slow him down one bit. It did, though, fill him with a fierce and frantic need to reach her bed—hell, *any* bed.

The first door on the left stood open in invitation and he rushed through it. Connor hardly noticed the room itself. All he saw was the double bed with the wrought iron head and foot rails. A colorful, flower-splashed quilt was spread over the mattress and a half dozen throw pillows in different colors and shapes were piled against the bigger bed pillows.

Every cell in his body urged him to hurry. To grab her, take her, fill himself with the taste and touch of her. Giving in to that urge, Connor flipped Emma over his shoulder and onto the mattress. She bounced a couple times and laughed even harder than she had downstairs.

"You're crazy," she said, grinning up at him in the moonlight pouring through the bedroom window overlooking the backyard.

"Been said before," he agreed, planting one knee on the edge of the bed and leaning over her.

She reached up and caught his face between her palms. Her gaze locked with his, and he felt as if she were trying to see all the way through him, down to his soul. And a part of him wondered what she'd find there.

Then philosophical questions faded from his mind as he slid one hand beneath the soft fabric of her tank top. At the first touch of her skin against his, he swallowed hard, and she hissed in a breath and let her eyes slide closed.

"Have to have you, Emma," he murmured, and bent his head to take one kiss, then two.

"Have to have each other," she answered, and snatched a kiss for herself as his hand slid higher, up her rib cage to cup her breast.

"No bra." The words slipped from him on a grateful sigh. His thumb and forefinger tweaked her pebbled nipple, and she arched into his touch, her breath sliding in and out of her lungs in hungry gasps.

Her skin was magic.

Warm silk.

He moved to straddle her body, his knees at her hips. He stared down at her as he pushed her tank top up and over her head, tearing it off and tossing it over his shoulder to land on the floor. A spill of moonlight lay across the bed and bathed Emma in a wash of pale light that almost made her skin glow.

He looked his fill and knew it would never be enough. He cupped her breasts in his hands and felt a hum of appreciation rush through him. Her nipples hardened at his touch. She reached up and ran her palms up and down his forearms, and he felt every stroke of her fingers like a live match against his skin.

Bending low, Connor indulged himself with a taste of her. He took first one nipple, then the other into his mouth, his tongue and teeth nibbling, pulling, teasing at her flesh until Emma was twisting and writhing beneath him.

Every move she made inflamed him. Every sigh that escaped her fed the flames engulfing him. Every touch made him want more. His eyes blurred, his brain shut down and his body took over. All he could think about was burying himself deep inside her. Feeling her damp heat surround him. Feeling her body quiver in climax.

He growled against her flesh and suckled her deeply. Emma's back bowed and she groaned his name as she clutched at his shoulders. "Connor, Connor don't stop. Don't stop doing that."

"Not a problem," he mumbled, surrendering to the hunger clawing at his insides. His mouth drew at her nipples again and again, feeling her need build, feeling his own desire ratchet up past the boil-over point, and still he wanted more.

Sliding down her body, he unzipped her shorts and as he moved, he skimmed them and the white lace panties beneath them, down and off her legs. In the moonlight, he saw the tan lines marking her body and felt his heart jump at the narrow strips of pale flesh over her breasts and at the juncture of her thighs. Why the thought of her in a tiny bikini could inflame him even while he was staring at her nudity, he couldn't figure out and didn't much care.

Everything he wanted in the world was there, at his fingertips. And he meant to enjoy it.

Emma felt him watching her and thought she might just burn to ashes under that heated gaze. But instead her body lit up like a fireworks display. His hands on her legs, as he caressed her from her ankles to her thighs and…oh, boy—even higher, felt hot, heavy, rough and so damn sensual, she couldn't imagine how she'd lived so long without having him touch her.

Her blood was bubbling inside. That had to be the reason why her whole body felt so twitchy. She wasn't a virgin. She'd had sex before.

But she'd never had sex like this before.

Not when she felt as though the top of her head was going to fly off into space—as though her insides were so jumbled with an intensifying need, that she might never feel normal again.

Connor's lips replaced his hands on her legs, and she felt the warmth of his breath dusting her skin as he moved to the insides of her thighs, kissing, nibbling, licking.

Her breath rushed in and out of her lungs. She heard herself panting. She felt herself writhing and couldn't stop. Didn't want to stop. All she wanted was more. More of *him*.

Then his mouth covered her center. "Connor!"

Thank heaven he didn't stop at her shout. She parted her thighs wider, inviting him closer. She planted her feet on the mattress and lifted her hips, rocking with the soul-shattering rhythm that he'd set with his lips and tongue. He tasted her intimately, sending showers of sparks throughout her body. Emma felt the world around her tremble as anticipation built within.

She opened her eyes and looked at him, watched him taste her, watched as he learned the secrets of her body, and she felt a rush of something hot and primal burst into life inside her.

His hands cupped her bottom and squeezed. She licked dry lips and kept her gaze locked on him as her body strained toward the shattering point that was now so close she could feel it.

Reaching down, she cupped the back of his head

and held him to her. Her fingers pushed through his silky black hair and she groaned as he nibbled at her. "Connor, I feel—I need—"

He growled.

No other word for it.

He seemed to know exactly what she needed. He growled against her body, lifted her hips in his strong hands, and as she dangled helplessly above the bed, he pushed her over the edge into a chasm so full of sparkling lights and colors, it nearly blinded her.

"Connor!" She shouted his name, heard the wildness in her own voice and reveled in it as she rode a climax unlike anything she'd ever known before.

As the last tremor rocked her body, he left her, and she wanted to weep for the loss. Her eyes closed to better savor the incredible wash of satisfaction sliding through her, she heard foil tearing and then he was there, somehow already gloriously naked, over her, filling her.

She arched her hips and took him inside. His body pushed into hers and the moment she felt his length within, she came again, trembling anew, riding fresh waves of pleasure that tore at her and left her gasping for air.

"Beautiful," he whispered, his voice a hush of sound in her ear. "So damn beautiful."

She *felt* beautiful. Emma grabbed him, holding him, her arms wrapped around him, her hands splayed against his back, pulling him tighter, closer.

She lifted her legs and hooked them around his waist, tilting her hips to take him even deeper.

He groaned as his hips rocked against hers in an age-old rhythm that sent flutters of brand-new need pulsing at the core of her. She met him, stroke for stroke, and enjoyed the feel of his body covering hers. The solid, heavy weight of him, pushing her down into the mattress. The ripple of muscles straining across his back.

Again and again he withdrew, then pushed himself home. Sweet friction escalated inside her, and Emma ran with it, eager to reach that peak one more time. The heady sound of flesh on flesh filled the room and became an intimate symphony.

He lifted his head to look down at her, and she gasped at the hunger glittering in his eyes. He looked like a warrior. Like the caveman he had pretended to be. He was intent. On *her*. On the breathless craving that had them both wrapped in a tight fist.

In the moonlight his broad, tanned chest looked delectable. She swept her hands around from his back and caressed his skin with her fingertips. At his flat nipples, she flicked the pebbled surface with her nails and watched as his eyes narrowed and his mouth flattened into a harsh line.

He grabbed her right hand, linked his fingers with hers and braced them both on the mattress. Staring down at her, he muttered thickly, "Come again, Em. Come with me this time."

As if his words alone had been enough to ignite

new flames, her body erupted, and bubbles of expectancy churned inside her. She moved with him again, feeling every sweep of his body against the so-tender flesh at the heart of her.

Again and again he staked his claim on her. Then he dipped his head and took her mouth with his. His tongue swept aside her defenses and claimed all that she was. His breath mingled with hers until she didn't know where she began and he ended and didn't care, either.

She tasted his need.

She shared his greed.

And this time when the world around them tottered and fell, they were together as they took the leap and together still when they fell.

# Eight

Connor's weight pressed Emma into the mattress, making each breath an adventure. But she didn't mind. In fact, she loved the feel of him lying atop her.

She loved the hum still vibrating inside her body. She loved how he made her feel when he touched her. She loved touching him and seeing his response flicker in his eyes.

And she was using the word love way too many times.

She put a mental stop to that real fast. Opening her eyes, Emma stared blindly up at the ceiling and tried to get a grip on the emotions churning through her. But it wasn't easy. Connor's breath labored in her ear and his heartbeat raced in tandem with her own. And she wondered if his stomach was suddenly doing a weird little pitch and roll.

Probably not.

Guys didn't spend a lot of time thinking about the repercussions of sex. Guys only thought about *getting* sex, and then once they'd had it, they worried about getting it *again*. Life was simpler for the Y chromosome set.

But as far as Emma was concerned, things had just gotten really complicated.

"I'm smashing you."

"Only a little." Stupid. She shouldn't have said that. Should have said, Yes, you are. Move over. But she hadn't wanted him to move and what did that say? Oh, God, she wasn't sure she wanted to know what that said.

Instantly the memory of Father Liam's warning came crashing back at her, echoing over and over again in her mind. Something about "being careful because sometimes even the best-laid traps snapped shut on the wrong target."

She squeezed her eyes shut and deliberately shut down the memory. Her trap had worked fine. Just as she'd planned. She'd gotten him into bed, hadn't she? She'd proven to Connor that she was as female as the next woman and she'd made sure he'd lost that stupid bet with his brothers.

No problem.

She squelched a groan. So if everything was so great, why wasn't she celebrating?

Connor lifted his head and, poised above her, he blocked her view of the ceiling and forced her to meet his gaze. She stared up at him and her heart gave a slow jolt that shuddered through her body like ripples on the surface of a pond.

*Oh, boy.*

"Damn, Emma..." His voice trailed off as he brushed a stray lock of blond hair off her forehead.

His features were stamped with an expression of stunned surprise, and Emma wasn't sure whether to be flattered or insulted. And did it really matter?

"That was—" he stopped and grinned "—amazing."

Oh, yeah, it had been, she thought, feeling the power of his smile slam into her. Amazing, earth-shattering, completely befuddling. Emma squelched a groan that was building deep inside her. She didn't want to put hearts and flowers on this night. That wasn't what this had been about.

She wasn't in love with Connor Reilly.

Didn't *want* to be in love with him.

That wasn't in the plan.

She'd set out to make him lose that bet for being so damn insulting, and she'd succeeded. That's all she had to remember here. That her scheme had worked. She'd brought him to his knees—figuratively speaking—and okay, she thought as she remembered him kneeling between her thighs, literally, too. But that was it. It was over.

And she'd be doing herself a huge favor to keep that in mind.

In an attempt to do just that, she forced a smile she didn't really feel and gave his back a friendly slap. "So, guess I'm not just 'one of the guys' after all, am I?"

He frowned down at her and levered himself up onto his elbows, taking most of his weight off her. Emma would rather have curled up and died than admit she missed the feel of his body pressed onto hers.

"One of the guys?" he echoed.

"You remember," she prodded, reminding herself as well as him. "A week or so ago we were talking about the bet and you said I was 'safe to hang out with'?"

"I did?" The frown on his face deepened and he shifted position slightly.

Emma swallowed another groan that erupted when his body, still locked within hers, stirred into life again.

Keep your mind on the conversation at hand, she warned herself. Keep remembering that, until about twenty minutes ago he hadn't really considered you a woman. "Yeah. You did."

He moved one hand to fiddle with the rubber band at the end of her braid. But she refused to be distracted.

*"And,"* Emma said, her breath hitching as his hips rocked against her, "you actually said, 'you're not a woman, Em…you're a *mechanic.'"*

"Huh."

She reminded him of the most humiliating moment of her life and all he had to say was *"huh*?"

His fingers undid her long, blond braid, and a part

of her brain focused on the soft tug as he freed her hair. But mostly she kept reminding herself that she'd won a victory here. A victory for every woman— heck, every *girl*—who was just a little bit different from the rest of the crowd.

"Don't you remember?" she demanded.

"Not really."

"But you said it," Emma insisted, determined now to ignore the stirring of her body as he shifted position over her again.

"If you say so."

"If *I* say so?" She blinked up at him and paid no attention when he pulled her now-loosened hair across her shoulders and dipped his head to bury his face in the thick mass. "Seriously, you don't remember saying that?"

"Vaguely," he said, and moved again, this time trailing warm, damp kisses along the line of her throat.

*"Vaguely?"*

"Do you really want to talk right now?" he mumbled, his words muffled against her neck.

No, she didn't want to talk. Didn't want to think. Didn't want to do anything except revel in the soft slide of his tongue along the length of her throat. She arched into him, despite her best efforts, and tilted her head to one side, giving him easier access. He smiled against her skin.

A sigh of a breeze drifted through the partially opened window and carried the scent of summer roses with it. The night was soft, quiet, as if she and Connor were the only two people in the world. It was as if they were wrapped together in a cocoon of sensation.

He was distracting her.

And doing a damn fine job of it, too. But they were getting off subject. She was trying to tell him that she'd tricked him into losing his precious bet, and he was too busy stirring her body up again to listen.

Determined now, Emma put both hands on his shoulders and shoved. He lifted his head and looked down at her, one corner of his mouth tugging into a half smile that did some incredible things to her insides. But Emma fought that reaction down and met his gaze steadily.

"What's wrong now?" he asked, and his deep voice rolled through the room like summer thunder.

"Nothing's *wrong*," she said tightly. "It's just—" How was she supposed to have a conversation with a man whose body was even now swelling to fill hers again? Concentrate, she thought. It was the only way. "Connor, I'm trying to tell you that I got you into bed deliberately. I *tricked* you."

"Yeah?" He smiled again and gave her a wink. "Then, thanks." Dipping his head, he took one of her nipples into his mouth and suckled it briefly.

She hissed in a breath as white-hot sensation shot through her bloodstream like skyrockets. Her vision blurred, her breath went soft and hazy, and she had to fight to come up for air again. When she did, she gave his broad, muscled shoulders another shove for good measure. "You're not listening to me."

"I'd rather kiss you," he admitted as he reluctantly lifted his head to stare down at her. "I'd rather taste you again. Why the sudden need for chitchat?"

His eyes seemed to glisten with a new urgency. And as he spoke, Emma felt her own heartbeat quicken in anticipation. But before they indulged themselves again, there were a few things that had to be said.

"Don't you get it, Connor?" she said, capturing his face between her palms. "I deliberately trapped you. Set you up, then knocked you down."

A short, sharp laugh shot from his throat. "Am I supposed to be sorry?"

"You lost the bet," she reminded him.

He frowned. "Oh, yeah…"

"I *wanted* you to lose the bet."

"Why?"

"To teach you a lesson," she said, and slid her hands from his cheeks, to his neck, to his shoulders, skimming over the hard, warm muscles and loving the feel of his skin beneath her palms. "To show you that just because I'm a mechanic doesn't make me less of a female."

He stared at her for a long moment, then slowly, a deep throated chuckle rumbled from his throat. "Well, you sure as hell proved your point, Em. I'm convinced," he said, still smiling as he dipped his head for a quick, hard kiss.

"Aren't you mad?"

"Should I be?" In one smooth move, he flipped onto his back, bringing her with him as he rolled over the mattress.

"You lost the bet."

"Seems like."

"I tricked you."

"Did an excellent job of it, too."

Straddling him now, Emma felt the thick, solid length of him pulsing within her. Unconsciously she rocked her hips and smiled when he hissed in air through clenched teeth. Watching him, she looked for signs of anger in his expression, but there was nothing there. He wasn't angry about losing the bet. Wasn't mad about being tricked.

What he *was,* was insatiable.

Thank heaven.

"But the money, Connor," she persisted. "It was down to just you and Aidan."

He reached up and covered her breasts with his hands, squeezing, rubbing, tweaking at her sensitized nipples until Emma moaned and let her head fall back.

"You think I give a damn about the bet now?"

Breathing hard, she lifted her head again and looked at him. "You don't?"

Shaking his head, he said, "I never would've made it, Em." He grinned. "Not hanging around you, anyway. And hell, it's hard to mind losing a bet when losing's this much fun."

She shrugged, and her hair slid over her skin like golden silk. "There is that."

He lifted his hips and Emma gasped as she rose up high, like a bronc rider astride a wild mustang. Except this felt *much* better. Her brain went on automatic pilot, and every inch of her body was already alert and screaming for attention.

Still, though, she couldn't leave things as they were. She had to know one more thing.

"Connor, where do we go from here?"

He stopped moving beneath her and locked his gaze with hers. His hands dropped to her hips and held her tightly, every finger pressing into her skin as if somehow branding her—however temporarily.

"Why do we have to go anywhere?" His voice was low, soft and she had to strain to hear him over the thundering crash of her own heartbeat. "Why does this have to be more than one night of amazing sex?"

If there was a part of her that was disappointed in his reaction, she buried it. After all, she hadn't been looking for a commitment. She hadn't been looking for *love*. She'd already tried love once and that had turned into a disaster of near epic proportions.

She'd never planned on having more than this one night with him. Her imagination hadn't taken her quite so far as that.

So Emma told herself to be grateful that Connor was who he was. A friend. A friend who happened to have the ability to turn her blood into steam...but a friend, first and foremost.

"It doesn't," she said, and deliberately twisted her hips, grinding her center against him, taking his body deeper, higher within her own. Her whole system shivered and she shook with the force of it. When she could speak again, she said, "One night, right? We have this one night and then go back to the way we were?"

He sucked in a gulp of air, his eyes fired in the shadows and then he nodded. "We stay friends."

"Friends," she agreed, and went up on her knees, feeling his body slide free of hers before she sank on him again, enjoying the rich feel of his hard length invading her heat.

Connor watched her as she moved over him and lost himself in the glory of the moment. How the hell could he think about where they went from here? How could he possibly worry about losing that stupid bet when Emma was riding him in slow, sensuous movements?

Her hair, loose and free, streamed over her shoulders and across her breasts, her rigid nipples peeking through the golden strands to tempt him. She was more beautiful than he could have imagined. She was more *everything* than he had ever guessed.

Her body was hot and tight, surrounding his with a velvety grip that drove him to the edge of oblivion with every move she made. He bit back a groan and choked off the urge to surrender to the climax crashing within. He wanted this to last. Wanted to stretch out their time together, to make the most of every second he spent here in her room.

Tomorrow he'd confess to his brothers that he'd lost the bet. Tomorrow things would go back to the way they'd always been between him and Emma. They'd be friends, because her friendship was something he didn't want to lose. But tonight they were different. Tonight they were lovers, and he for damn sure meant to enjoy every minute of it.

She arched her back and moaned, a soft sigh of sound that shook him down to his bones. He tightened his grip on her hips and increased the rhythm sparking between them. Over and over again, she pulled free of his body only to capture him again with a nearly hypnotic effect.

Moonlight danced on her naked flesh and she let her head fall back again as she rode him. He felt his own release building and knew he wouldn't be able to hold out much longer. His breath staggered from heaving lungs. His brain was short-circuiting. His body felt electrified—surging with a power he'd never known before.

And Connor knew he wanted to take Emma with him when his body exploded. Dropping one hand to the spot where their bodies joined, he stroked her damp heat. Rubbed the one spot on her body that he knew would send her tumbling wildly over the edge.

"Connor…" She said his name on a throaty groan of need and passion.

He continued to stroke her, watching as her features shifted with the churning emotions slashing at her. She moved faster, rocking her hips with him in a timeless rhythm that swept both of them up in a frantic rush toward completion.

And when her body splintered, he caught her and held on as he let himself follow after.

"I'm out." Connor slid onto the bench seat at the Lighthouse Diner and shrugged when all three of his brothers just stared at him.

He hadn't been looking forward to this. Facing his brothers and admitting that he hadn't been able to last the full three months of their bet was humiliating. Even though, he thought, with a small inner smile, losing the bet had been the best time of his life.

When that thought crowded into his brain, Connor frowned and pushed it back out.

"You're kidding, right?" Aidan, sitting right beside him asked, with an elbow jab to his ribs.

"Ow." Connor looked from Aidan to Brian and finally to Liam. "Nope. Not kidding. I'm out. Fit me for the coconut bra."

"Woo-hoo!" Aidan hooted gleefully and signaled the waitress to bring another round of beers to the table. Shifting his gaze back to his brothers, he grinned and said, "This round's on me. In celebration."

"Hey," Connor reminded him, "just because I lost, doesn't mean *you* won."

"He's right," Brian chimed in. "We're out of the running, but you signed on for three whole months of no sex. You've still got another six weeks to go, man."

"Piece o' cake," Aidan said, reaching for the bowl of tortilla chips in the center of the table. "I'll show you guys how it's done."

"Right," Liam said, sarcasm dripping from his tone. "You're in complete control."

"Totally," Aidan boasted.

"Liar," Brian said, taking a sip of his beer.

"Hey," Aidan took exception. "Shouldn't you guys be ragging on Connor? *He's* the one who lost the bet, y'know."

"Thanks," Connor said, and absently smiled at the waitress as she brought them each a tall, frosty glass of beer. He took a long drink and let the icy, foamy drink slide through him, cooling him off.

It had been a long, hot day.

And every time his thoughts had returned to the night before, spent in Emma's arms, the temperature had only climbed.

"So," Liam asked in the sudden silence, "do we get to know who?"

Connor glanced up from his drink and found all three of his brothers watching him. Well, hell. Only a few weeks ago he'd sat in this very booth and laughed his tail off as Brian had confessed to dropping out of the bet. Funny, it had seemed hilarious at the time. Now...not so much.

"Emma," he said tightly.

"The mechanic?" Aidan's voice hitched in surprise.

A flicker of something hot and dangerous sparked into life inside Connor. He swiveled his head to stare at the brother sitting alongside him through narrowed eyes. "You've got a problem with Emma?" he asked tightly. "Something wrong with her?"

Aidan's eyes widened as he lifted both hands in mock surrender and shook his head. "Nope, not a thing. I was just surprised is all. Chill out, man."

"A little touchy aren't you?" Brian asked.

"And your point is…" Connor demanded, sparing the man opposite him a quelling look.

"No point, just an observation."

"Emma's a sweetheart," Liam's quiet voice spoke up, and the three men looked at him. Liam shrugged. "Hey, she fixes my car and I think she's cute."

Brian lifted one eyebrow and chuckled. "You *are* a priest, remember?"

"I'm a priest, I'm not dead." Liam shook his head and then turned to focus on Connor. "So you and Emma are together now?"

Panic reared up inside Connor. He leaned back into the booth, as if to distance himself as much as possible from that question. "Together? No. We're not a couple or anything. We're just friends."

"*Naked* friends," Aidan said on a laugh.

"Best kind." Brian lifted his beer in salute.

"Friendships change," Liam mused quietly.

Connor slanted him a wary glance. It didn't help at all that he himself had been thinking the same damn thing all day. His friendship with Emma was important to him. They got along great, shared a love of cars and old movies and thunderstorms. They could talk about anything, and he trusted her as he trusted few other people in his life.

Connor's friends were important to him.

And Emma was a *friend*.

"Whatever you're thinking," he grumbled, "just forget about it. I'm not looking to get married like poor ol' Bri here."

"Hey," Brian objected. "It's not like I'm caught in a trap trying to chew my leg off to get free, you know."

"I didn't say that," Connor snapped. "I just said that it wasn't for me." Never had been, never would be. He didn't want to be married. Didn't want to have anyone depending on him. Didn't want to change who he was to accommodate someone else.

He liked his life just the way it was. Hot and cold running women streaming in and out of his life in a constantly shifting smorgasbord of femininity.

Emma was a great woman—but she wasn't going to be the *only* woman.

That's not what he was looking for.

Connor waved Brian off and concentrated on his brother the priest. "Don't start thinking that just because Emma and I heated up the sheets that it's going to be anything more than that, Liam."

"I don't know, bro," Aidan pointed out, helping himself to another chip, "you *did* give up a shot at ten thousand bucks for her."

Connor scraped one hand across his face and wished to hell he'd been born an only child. "It was just sex."

"You sure?" Liam asked quietly.

"Of course I'm sure." Connor picked up his beer and took a long swallow. As the conversation between his brothers went on without him, he fought down the stray thought niggling in the back of his mind.

The one that claimed he wasn't as sure as he was pretending to be.

# Nine

<u>Nine</u>

"**M**rs. Harrison," Emma said as she stalked around the confines of her small office, tethered by the coiled phone cord. "If you'd just reconsider, I could make you a very good offer for the car."

The woman on the other end of the phone line sighed, then said, in a soft, Southern drawl, "I know it seems silly to you, Emma dear, but I just can't bear to part with Sonny's car. He loved it so."

"But that's my point, Mrs. Harrison," Emma plunked down on the one uncluttered corner of her desk and stared off through the front windows at Main Street. "If Sonny loved the car so much, wouldn't he want to see it restored to all its former glory?"

"Well…"

While the older woman thought about that, Emma stared out at Baywater. Summer traffic was still as thick as the humid air. Even at sunset, tourists crowded the sidewalks and cars backed up at the streetlights. Horns blasted, people shouted, and kids, apparently immune to the heat, dashed along sidewalks on skateboards, dogs nipping and yelping at their sides.

A typical, ordinary, summer evening.

So why did everything feel so different?

Because *she* was different.

Emma sighed and told herself to get over it. To get past it. But how could she? For hours the night before, she and Connor had made love. It was as if neither of them could bear to stop touching the other. He'd stayed with her until sunrise, leaving only when the first streaks of crimson splashed the horizon.

She'd walked him to the door and watched him stride to his car and then drive away and she hadn't once given in to the urge to call him back.

But it had been there.

A crouched, needy thing deep inside her. She'd fought it back and made herself remember the promise they'd made to each other after their first bout of soul-shattering sex.

*Friends.*

They'd vowed to remain friends and she wanted that. Absolutely. But she also wanted him in her bed. And just how was she supposed to get past that?

Oh, things were fast getting more complicated instead of easier.

"I don't know, dear," Mrs. Harrison said, dragging Emma gratefully away from her thoughts. "It just doesn't seem quite right to me somehow."

Emma sighed, but she wasn't really surprised. She spoke to Mrs. Harrison at least once a month, hoping to get the woman to part with that old Corvette. Sonny Harrison had been dead for forty years, but his mother still wasn't ready to let his car—all she had left of him—go. So Emma would give up today and try again in a month.

"I understand," she said, and a part of her really did. It had to be hard, losing the one last link to a past that felt more real than the present. It was pretty much how she'd felt the day she'd packed up all of her girly clothes after her ex-fiancé, Tony Demarco, had shown his true colors. But she'd gotten over the death of her dreams, and one of these days maybe Mrs. Harrison would, too. "I hope you don't mind if I keep trying to convince you, though."

"Not at all, honey. You call again real soon."

When they hung up, Emma smiled. She had a feeling that the elderly woman would never sell her that car—mainly because then she'd lose the fun of Emma's phone calls and visits.

The phone rang again almost instantly, and for one brief shining moment, Emma thought that maybe Mrs. Harrison had changed her mind. "Hello? Jacobsen's Garage."

"You haven't called me with an update."

"Mary Alice?"

"Who else?"

Emma smiled, walked around the edge of her desk and sat down in her chair. Kicking her feet up, she crossed her legs at the ankle on top of a stack of papers at the edge of the desk and said, "I've been meaning to call you."

"Uh-huh," her friend said, "and I've been meaning to go on a diet."

"Another one?" Emma grinned.

"Let's not get off track here," Mary Alice said quickly. "This isn't about *me.* I want details. When last I heard, Mr. Gorgeous Reilly was walking up to your office looking like dessert."

"Oh, wow…"

"I'm guessing that this is going to be a long story?"

"You have no idea." She'd meant to call Mary Alice. She really had. But she'd gotten so involved with her own plans and preparations for snapping a trap shut on Connor, that Emma'd completely forgotten about everything but the task at hand.

And after the night before, she thought, her insides curdling into a warm puddle of something sticky, she was lucky she could think at all.

"So talk."

"Where do you want me to start?" Emma asked, "With the first time or the last time?"

Mary Alice sucked in a breath that was audible

even from three thousand miles away. "How many in between?"

"Three." Connor, Emma had learned during the long night, was a pretty amazing man. In stamina alone, the Marines were lucky to have him.

And so was she.

*Whoops.* A minor mental slip there.

She didn't actually *have* him, now did she?

"Oh, boy." A heavy sigh drifted through the phone line. "Hold on a sec."

A lot more than one second ticked past before Mary Alice spoke again. "Okay," she said. "I'm back. I needed a glass of wine for this. Start talking and remember to linger over the details."

Emma laughed and silently thanked her friend for calling when she most needed her. "God I love you."

"Ditto. Now spill your guts."

Connor'd had every intention of staying away.

He'd reassured himself all day long that there'd be no problem in keeping his distance. It was for the best, anyway. For both of them. Last night had been amazing, but it was one night out of their lives.

Emma was his friend. That she was also the woman who'd nearly set his hair on fire the night before, wasn't important. The friendship *was*. So with that thought firmly in mind, he'd made a solemn vow to himself that he'd steer clear of her for at least the next few days.

Give them both a little breathing room.

Make the memory of last night a little dimmer before they spent time together again.

After dinner with his brothers, he'd even driven halfway home before he'd found himself turning around and heading back to Emma's house. The disappointment he'd felt at seeing the house dark and empty wasn't something he wanted to think about. And what he should have done was take her absence as a sign from above. Someone up there was looking out for him. Steering him away from Emma even when he was trying to hunt her down.

Instead though, he'd driven to the garage.

Over the past two years, there had been plenty of times when he'd worked late with her, helping her with a stubborn oil change or just sitting in the office talking. In fact, he hadn't really noticed—until he started trying to stay away from her—just how much time he actually spent with Emma.

Somehow or other, when he wasn't looking, she'd become an integral part of his day. She was usually the one he complained to about whichever new recruit was giving him fits. She was the one he laughed with over the stories Aidan told. She was the one who listened to him grouse about his dates, his job, his life.

Emma was more than a friend.

She was his *best* friend.

"And now you know what she looks like naked." He groaned tightly and told himself to shut that thought off fast. No way could he concentrate on driving if his brain was filled with images of Emma's smooth skin in the moonlight.

Beside him at the stoplight, a carload of teenagers were whooping and hollering. The girls looked shiny bright and the boys were busy trying to be cool. Music blasted through their open windows and into Connor's, shattering his thoughts. He smiled to himself as the light changed and the car sped off with a squeal of rubber on asphalt. He almost envied them.

Summer nights were made for long drives and laughter. For stolen kisses and slow walks. For sighs and whispers and the promise of more.

And damn it, he *wanted* more.

More of Emma.

"You're in bad shape," he muttered grimly as he steered the car toward the garage. His fingers clenched the steering wheel until his knuckles were white. His stomach jumped and his brain was shouting at him to stay the hell away from Emma.

But he wasn't listening.

He couldn't.

Besides, he thought, staying away from her was probably not the answer. *Not* seeing her only made him think about her more. Maybe *seeing* her would help him keep this whole business in perspective.

That thought made him feel a little better about the whole situation. Slapping the steering wheel with the flat of his hand, he nodded and said, "Exactly. She's your friend. So going to see her is just proving to both of you that you can deal."

If a small voice in the back of his mind whispered that he was just making excuses…he ignored it.

He pulled into the parking lot in front of Jacobsen's Garage and noticed that the office was dark but that lights were on in the garage bay. The oversize garage door was closed, but the half-moon-shaped windows above the door shone with soft lamplight.

Turning the engine off, he set the brake, clenched his jaw and realized that for the first time in his life, he felt like retreating.

That thought alone was enough to get him out of the car and moving toward the shop. The hot summer night closed in around him as he stalked across the parking lot like a man on a mission.

Emma'd always liked working late. She liked being here alone. Having time to think, she called it, and Connor wondered what she was thinking about tonight.

Opening the office door, which she should have had locked, damn it, Connor scowled and closed it behind him, turning the lock for good measure. What the hell was she thinking, working late and leaving the door open for just anybody to stroll inside? His stomach fisted as the thought of "what might have beens" rushed through his brain.

Idiotic, he knew. Baywater was a safe, tiny community and no doubt there was nothing to worry about. But he suddenly didn't like the idea of Emma working here late at night, all alone. He suddenly didn't like the idea of her *being* alone. And what the hell did *that* mean? It hadn't bothered him last week or last month or last year. Oh, man—

Shaking his head, Connor stepped into the air-conditioned office and headed for the connecting door to the garage. A wave of hot, steamy air rushed at him. The garage was not air-conditioned, since it would have been impractical, with the door wide-open all day. There were fans whirring in every corner, but they didn't do much to reduce the ovenlike effect.

Connor didn't care, though. He stepped into the heat and closed the door to the office behind him. He heard the music first, and smiled in spite of the thoughts churning in his mind. Classic rock and roll, and if he knew Emma, she was singing along, safe in the knowledge that there was no one to hear her.

He paused in the shadows, giving himself time to simply admire the view.

She hadn't heard him come in—not surprising since the radio volume was set at just under ear shattering. She wore coverall—standard, gray coverall that before wouldn't have given him a moment's pause. Today, though, he wasn't fooled. Today he knew what kind of weapons she was hiding beneath the too-baggy work uniform. And his body went hard just thinking about it.

She did a quick little sidestep, her hips swaying to the rhythm pounding out around her and her blond ponytail swung with her movements. She kept time with the rhythm even as her small, capable hands worked on the carburetor lying in pieces on the workbench.

He grinned when she picked up a wrench and, holding it as if it were a microphone, sang into it along with the voice pouring from the radio. Even though she had more enthusiasm than talent, Emma poured her heart into the song of love and loss, and something inside Connor twisted as he watched her.

Beautiful.

Even in the ugly gray coverall, she was beautiful.

Sure, he thought. *Friends*. No problem here.

Scraping one hand across his face, Connor breathed deeply, hoping to ease the instinct clamoring within. The one that was prompting him to march across the garage, grab her up and bury himself inside her as fast as he could. Every cell in his body was on high alert.

Coming here had been a lousy idea.

But he couldn't have left if it had meant his life.

When she lifted both arms high and did a spin to coincide with the end of the song, she spotted him. Stopping dead, she squeaked out a half-choked-off scream and slapped one hand to her chest.

"Connor!" She took a deep, steadying breath, then blew it out in an exasperated rush. Reaching across the workbench, she hit the volume button on the radio and cranked it down to background level. "Geez, you scared me half to death. Do you have to be all stealthy?"

Stealthy? Hell, he was surprised she hadn't heard

his heart pounding over the blast of the radio. "Sorry. Didn't mean to surprise you."

"Next time say something."

"Like?"

"Like, hello?" Still agitated, she dropped the wrench onto the work surface, then rubbed her palms together. "How tough is that?"

Right now, he thought, pretty damn hard. Hard to talk at all past the knot of need lodged in his throat. But he forced a smile and said, "Fine. Hello, Emma."

She smiled, tipped her head to one side and studied him. "Something wrong?"

Hell, yes. He'd been thinking all day about getting his best friend naked again. That was wrong in so many ways.

But all he said was, "No."

"Didn't think I'd be seeing you today."

She wiped her hands on a clean rag, then tossed it onto the bench behind her. From the radio came a soft rush of guitars and drums, pulsing out around them.

"Yeah, me, neither."

She shoved her hands into the pockets of the coveralls. "So why are you here?"

Good question.

"Because we said we'd stay friends, Em. Because if I stay away from you because of last night, we'd lose that."

"True."

"And," he admitted, "I wanted to prove to myself

that I could come here—see you—and not want to take you to bed again."

She frowned at him and he could have sworn the temperature in the garage dropped a few degrees. "Gee, that just makes me feel all warm and fuzzy."

"That probably came out wrong," he muttered.

"You think?"

"Damn it, Emma." He started across the garage toward her. He closed the distance between them with four long strides that took him around the front end of the sleek little convertible waiting to be serviced. When he was right on top of her, he stared down into her eyes. "This is new territory for me, ya know? I generally don't spend a lot of time thinking about getting my friends naked."

She grinned, and he felt the power of that smile reach in and grab his throat.

"Good to know."

"The point is," he said, letting his gaze slide across her features, from her tiny, straight nose to the curve of her mouth and back up to the depths of her eyes. He inhaled and blew the air out again in a rush. "The point is, I *am* thinking about getting you naked. And I'm thinking about it *way* too much."

She shivered and he fisted his hands at his sides to keep from reaching for her. If he touched her now, that would be it. No going back, no reining in, no turning away.

"So stop," she said, lifting her chin.

"Easier said than done."

"Yeah," she said on a sigh, "I know."

The tight, cold fist around his lungs eased back a little. "You, too?"

"Only every other minute or so." She backed up from him, as if just talking about this was getting a little too difficult. "But it'll pass. Right?"

"Shown no signs so far." He kept pace with her, taking one step forward for each of her backward steps.

"Only been a day."

"A *whole* day," he said.

"Right." She glanced around the shop as if looking for the nearest exit, then caught herself and stopped at the front end of the red sports car. "Twenty-four whole hours."

He nodded and moved in closer. "Thousands of minutes."

"Uh-huh." She licked her lips and stared up at him. "We're gonna do it again, aren't we?"

"Oh, yeah." He wanted her with everything in him. He'd never known such all-consuming hunger before, and a part of him wondered if it would always be this way. Was there no going back to the way things had been between him and Emma? Did he really *want* to go back?

Hell, no.

But at the same time Connor was forced to admit that if they couldn't go back, they'd have to go forward. There was no standing still.

Though maybe there *could* be. Just for tonight. Tomorrow was soon enough to think about the repercussions. Tonight all he wanted to do was recapture those hours he'd had with her the night before. Wanted to lose himself in the taste of her, surround himself with her heat and watch as her eyes glazed over with pleasure.

Everything else could just wait.

He bent, grabbed her up and kissed her, long and hard and deep. His tongue swept into her warmth and claimed another piece of her soul. Her breath mingled with his. Her tongue teased his. Her heartbeat shuddered in time with his own and when she arched into him, Connor's mind emptied of everything but the raging need pounding inside him.

Desperate to touch her, to have her, he reached for the zipper at the front of her coveralls and whispered, "I've gotta know what you're wearing under this thing."

Her eyes went wide. She grabbed his hands and held them still.

"What?" He met her gaze and saw embarrassment dart across the surface of her eyes. "What's wrong?"

"Nothing," she hedged, and lowered her gaze, still keeping a tight grip on his hands. "It's just…"

"Tell me."

She took a deep breath and forced herself to look up at him. "Fine. When I shut the garage bay doors, it was really hot in here and—well, I was all alone and—you know," she pointed out, "the shop was closed…"

"Will you just spit it out?"

Emma let go of his hands and huffed out a breath. "Fine. It's hot in here, so…"

"So?" Impatience clawed at him.

"So, I'm not wearing *anything* under it."

Connor's blood rushed through his veins. His body went hard and tight and eager. His breath staggered in his lungs. Looking down into her flushed face, he smiled and took hold of the zipper again. Giving it a tug, he stared at her lusciously delectable, completely naked body beneath those ugly gray coveralls and smiled as he whispered, "It's Christmas."

Emma laughed, but the sound ended abruptly as his hands covered her breasts. Thumbs and forefingers squeezed, tweaked and pulled at her nipples. She gasped and felt the drawing sensation right down to the soles of her feet.

From the corners of the room, fans pushed hot air at them, and still Emma felt as though she couldn't catch her breath. His hands. She'd been daydreaming about his hands all day and now suddenly, they were here, on her, driving her up that wild, slippery slope that led to an amazing reward.

"Gotta have you, Em," he murmured thickly as he leaned over her, pushing her back, back, until she lay atop the hood of the red convertible.

"Need you, Connor. Right now. Oh, please," she whispered as his mouth closed over one of her nipples, *"right now."*

His right hand dipped down her body, sliding

across her abdomen, past the nest of tight curls at her center until he touched the heart of her. Light, skimming strokes pushed her higher, faster, than she'd ever been before. And still it wasn't enough.

"Now, Connor," she begged and even hearing the pleading in her own voice couldn't stop her from begging again. "I want you inside me. Now."

"Right now, baby." He lifted his head, pulled his hand free of her heat and reached for the shoulders of her coveralls. In one slick move, he'd scooped the fabric off her shoulders, down the length of her body and off. Then he was laying her back against the hood of the car and all she could think was, the metal still felt cool against her skin. Despite the hot air and the heat he created within her, the metal was cool and slick beneath her body.

Emma opened her eyes and watched him as he quickly undid his jeans and stepped out of them. Pulling his shirt off, he came to her, strong, muscular, tanned and ready. Emma's hands itched to touch him, to scrape her fingernails down his back and over the curve of his behind. She wanted to feel him atop her. Feel him fill her until all the lonely, empty spaces inside were quiet.

She licked her lips as if awaiting a treat, and he caught the motion and gave her a slow smile. Grabbing a condom from his wallet, he tore the paper open, smoothed the fragile rubber over himself and came to her. She lifted her legs, parting them wide in welcome and held her breath as he entered her on a sigh.

The radio played, a fast, pulsing tune that gave them the rhythm they both needed. Fast, hard, hungry. Again and again, they parted and rejoined as he plunged within her and each time was harder, stronger, more relentless than the last.

And as the end crashed down around them, Connor looked down into her eyes, and Emma lost herself in his dark-blue gaze. She cried out his name as the heat swallowed them and bound them even more tightly together.

# Ten

"**O**kay," Emma said as soon as she was able to talk without her voice quavering, "this was a mistake."

"Hard to look at it like that when you're in my position," Connor quipped and grinned down at her.

That grin was such a potent weapon. And with his body still pressed to hers, still intimately invading hers, she could hardly argue the point. *However*, one of them had to make a stand—even if she was lying down when she did it.

"Get up, Connor."

"What's your hurry?" He nibbled at her throat, then deliberately ran his tongue across her skin.

Bubbles of fresh anticipation frothed to life inside her. She could almost hear her blood boiling. Every inch of her body felt alert, awake, *alive*—all because of him. How had they managed to know each other for two years and never discover the chemistry that lay sizzling between them? And how could they get back to where they'd been, now that they *had* discovered it?

Emma's stomach jittered at the thought that maybe they wouldn't be able to go back. Maybe by finding something special, they'd lost something equally important. She closed her eyes and bit back a groan. Then, gritting her teeth, she said, "I mean it, Connor," and slapped one hand against his back for emphasis. "Get up."

"Bossy little thing, aren't you?" he asked, lifting his head to look down at her again. A self-satisfied half smile curved his mouth, and it was all she could do to keep from reaching up and defining that curve with her fingertips.

"How come I never noticed that about you before?"

"There are a lot of things you didn't notice."

"Yeah," he wiggled his eyebrows and leered at her. "But I'm catching on quick."

He rocked his hips against her, and her bones melted—along with what little resolve she'd been able to muster. Before she succumbed completely, though, she ordered, "Connor…"

"I'm moving, I'm moving."

He did. Slowly, tantalizingly. As if he were tormenting her for ending this little…*session*.

Emma stifled a groan and bit down on her bottom

lip to keep from asking him to stay. To make love to her again. Oh, she had to be out of her mind. Here she had a gorgeous, talented lover at her disposal and she was telling him thanks but no thanks?

Her brain screamed at her to be rational, and her body was shouting just as loudly to stop thinking and just feel. She wasn't sure which of them was the stronger at the moment, so as soon as she could, Emma slid off the hood of the car and quickly grabbed up her coveralls. With clothing, might come clear thinking. Heaven knew it wasn't there when she was naked.

The fans blew a constant stream of heated air against her sweat-dampened skin, and chills rippled along her spine. She shivered and kept moving.

Stepping into her clothes again, Emma kept her back to Connor until she was dressed, with the zipper pulled up to her throat. Stupid, since he'd already seen her naked, but hey, she needed all the armor she could get at the moment. Shoving the oversize sleeves up to her elbows, she took a deep breath, ignored the hum still reverberating throughout her body and turned around to face him.

He had his jeans on, but he was still bare-chested, and a more tempting sight Emma couldn't imagine. Her mouth watered and she felt her resistance melting like ice in a warm drink. Oh, she'd really opened up a huge can of worms by starting all this. And if she could have figured out how to do it, she would have kicked her own behind.

They'd been happy. Fine. Good friends. Then she'd let herself get all huffy and offended, and now see where they'd landed. Up a creek without even a boat—let alone a paddle. And she had absolutely no idea how to undo it.

Or even if she wanted to.

And that one thought worried her.

Because she was slipping.

She could feel it.

Her heart ached, just looking at him. If the situation were different—if *she* were different, she might have allowed herself a little dreaming. Might have let what she already felt for him blossom. Might have indulged in the hopes and fantasies that she'd once believed in.

But fantasies were fragile, and dreams were tricks your mind played on you. She knew that. She'd learned her lesson the hard way. So she ached at the knowledge that nothing would ever be the same between Connor and her again.

Their easy friendship was gone, burned in a fire she hadn't expected to find.

"Whatever you're thinking," he said softly, "it looks serious."

"What?"

"Should I be worried?" He yanked his dark-red T-shirt over his head and shoved his arms through the sleeves.

"One of us should be," she murmured. Then louder she said, "We can't keep doing this."

He grinned again. "Give me five minutes, I think I could change your mind."

No doubt he could. But that wasn't the point. "Connor, I'm trying to do the right thing, here."

"Well, cut it out." Scowling, he reached over and flipped off the radio. With the music suddenly cut off, the whir of the fans was the only sound as they faced each other.

Emma could have sworn she could actually *see* electricity flashing back and forth between them. Heaven knew she felt the heat. But she closed her heart to it. Sighing, she said, "Last night was a bump in the road."

"More than one," he commented wryly.

She ignored it. "But tonight just proves that this is getting out of hand."

Scowling, he said, "Okay, I admit, things got a little out of hand tonight—"

"Yeah, just a little."

He shook his head and folded his arms over his chest. He braced his long legs in a wide apart, battle stance and Emma wondered idly who he was preparing to fight? Her? Or himself?

"You should know this isn't why I came here tonight."

Of course she knew that. After all, no one would *plan* to have sex on the hood of a car. She sighed again. "I know, it's just—"

"I came to talk since I couldn't find you at home," he continued, cutting her off neatly. "And, hey—" he broke off and glared down at her "—by the way, lock the damn door when you're here alone, Emma."

"Excuse me?"

"The door to the shop. It was unlocked. For God's sake, anybody could have come in."

"Anybody did," she said, stiffening in self-defense.

"Yeah, but you *know* me."

"I used to think so."

"What's *that* supposed to mean?" he demanded.

Temper flared into life inside her, and Emma clung to it desperately. Anger was easier to deal with than whatever it was she was feeling for Connor at the moment. "It means that whether or not I lock my doors is up to *me*."

"Who the hell said it wasn't?" He unfolded his arms and threw his hands high as if trying to catch the threads of the argument that were quickly spiraling out of his control.

"You did," she snapped, folding her own arms across her chest and glaring back at him. This was comfort. This was safety. An argument with Connor she could handle. Tenderness from him left her wary and unsure of herself. "I'm perfectly safe here."

He frowned at her, his dark-blue eyes getting nearly frosty. "Probably," he admitted. "But it's stupid to take chances, Emma."

"I'm not stupid, and I don't need you to tell me what to do."

He gaped at her. "I didn't say you were stupid."

"You did, too, just a minute ago."

"I said it was stupid not to lock the door."

"And since I didn't, I'm stupid."

"What the hell's going on with you, Emma?" His voice growled out with the strength and ferocity of a grizzly bear coming out of winter hibernation, looking for a meal.

She didn't *know.* God help her, she just didn't know. Thoughts, emotions, feelings, splintered inside her and the slippery shards were too fragile…too many to identify. All she knew for sure was that she needed to be alone. She needed to think. Desperately she fought to control the rising sense of panic clawing at her insides. "I don't like being ordered around."

He sucked in a huge gulp of air, swallowed it and paused, as if silently counting to ten. Or twenty. Emma could have told him it wouldn't help. She'd already tried it.

Finally he spoke again, keeping his voice low and even. "I'm not *telling* you what to do. I'm just saying I was worried when I saw you were vulnerable and—"

Oh, she was plenty vulnerable. But not in the way he meant. Everything inside her was a churning, dazzling swirl of need and fury. She wanted him and couldn't have him. Needed him and didn't want to. Loved him and—

*Oh, God.*

She staggered back a step.

Felt the blood drain from her head until the room tilted ominously.

*She loved Connor Reilly.*

Air rushed in and out of her lungs in short, sharp gasps. The edges of her vision sparkled with white and blue dots, and she wondered absently if this is what an out-of-body experience felt like. For a second or two she worried that she might faint. Then the thought of waking up and having to explain to Connor just what had prompted the faint quickly slapped her back into shape.

Heat pulsed inside her, then was rapidly replaced by an icy chill that made her shiver reflexively.

*Love?*

OhGodohGodohGod.

Trouble. Big trouble.

No way out.

She slapped one hand to her forehead and rubbed at the sudden throbbing of a massive headache. But it wasn't going anywhere. Her brain felt as if it were about to explode. Her mouth was dry, it hurt to swallow and still she had to speak. Had to say something to keep him from noticing that she was currently in the middle of a minor nervous breakdown.

She pulled in a shaky breath and blew it out before trying to speak. "I'm not *yours* to worry about Connor."

How did the man go from smoldering lover to scolding big brother in ten seconds flat? And for pity's sake, how could she *love* him for it?

"I-didn't-say-that." Each word was bitten off as if it tasted bitter. "All I said was—"

She held up one hand and tried not to notice that it was shaking. Then, curling her fingers into her palm, she said, "I heard you the first time. But whether or not I lock the door is no concern of yours."

He was right, though, and that only made her madder. She never worked late without locking herself in the garage. Baywater was safe, she knew, but she didn't take foolish chances. And if she *had* locked the stupid door, then Connor couldn't have sneaked up on her, they wouldn't have made love again and *she* wouldn't have had to face the completely startling fact that she'd gone and fallen in love.

"Now I can't worry about you?"

She shot him a hard look, fired by the anger rippling through her at her own stupidity. "Did you worry *before* we went to bed together?"

He started to speak, then closed his mouth again. But then, she didn't need to hear his answer. She already knew what it was.

"No, you didn't," she said for him. Fury pulsed wildly inside her, like a living, breathing creature, completely separate from her. He was just like Tony, she thought frantically. This was déjà vu and she didn't want to go back there. Didn't want to remember the pain, the disappointment, the regret of having loved someone who couldn't or wouldn't understand her.

Like Tony, Connor wasn't seeing the *real* her.

"When we were just friends," she said hotly, "you

assumed I could take care of myself. Now that we've been naked together, apparently I've lost a few brain cells."

"Damn it, Em," he took a step toward her, then stopped dead. "I didn't say that, either."

"You didn't have to," she snapped. "I can see it in your face. God, Connor, it's practically stamped on your forehead."

"What're you talking about?"

"You. Me. *This*." She waved one hand at the car where they'd just made love and nearly shivered. But she stiffened her spine instead. "I've been down this road before, Connor. Trust me, I'm not going to do it again."

"What's that mean?"

"You're just like Tony."

He threw his hands high. "Who the hell's *Tony?*"

"I was engaged to him three years ago."

He blinked at her. His expression was thunderstruck. He looked like a man who'd just been pummeled with a two by four and wasn't sure whether to stagger or fall down.

"Engaged?" He repeated after a moment or two. "You were *engaged?* Why didn't I know about this?"

"You never asked."

He opened his mouth, then snapped it shut again.

She shook her head and stared up at him, too wound up to be quiet now, even if that might have been the better thing to do. "You're just like him, I swear. He never noticed me until I wore girly clothes.

Just like you, Connor. And when I was just *me*, he wasn't interested. He even wanted me to sell the garage. Become the perfect little wife who baked cookies and drove in car pools. Well, there's nothing wrong with that, but it's not *me*."

"And I'm like that moron exactly *how?*"

"Oh, please," she said, on a roll now and unwilling to quit. "You never looked twice at me until that night at the bar."

"That doesn't—"

She cut him off, unwilling to listen to lame-ass excuses. "When I'm a woman, you want to protect me. When I'm *me*, that all changes. Well, guess what, Connor? I'm the same person. Whether I'm in a skirt or these coveralls."

"I know that—"

"I don't think you do. I think you're all hot and bothered over the girly Emma. Well, that's not who I am, Connor." She waved a hand at the grease-spattered coveralls. "*This* is me. The real me. And she's not someone you'd go for. Face it."

"So now you read minds?"

She choked out a laugh. "Yours isn't that hard to read."

Darn it, everything was falling apart. Just like she'd known it would. She never should have let this get started. Never should have tried to set him up, because in doing so, she'd knocked the earth out from under her own feet and now she was on shaky ground.

And the fact that a part of her almost wished she

were the girly-girl type—the kind of woman that Connor would want—really irritated her.

"So you've got this all figured out," he said tightly.

"You bet."

"You get engaged to a jerk and then figure every other guy is just like him?"

"Not every guy."

"Just me."

She nodded, not trusting herself to speak.

"The man was an idiot."

"Yeah," Emma said, "but at least he was honest about what he wanted. You're not being honest, Connor. Not with me. Not with yourself."

"That's just perfect," he muttered, shoving both hands along the sides of his head as if trying to keep his skull from exploding.

Well, she knew just how he felt. Funny how the warm, delicious buzz she'd been feeling only a few moments ago had completely faded away. Now all that was left was a sense of loss.

And just a touch of mind-numbing panic.

"You should probably just go, Connor."

"Not till we talk about this."

She laughed and the sound of it was shrill, even to her. "We've been talking, Connor. And we're going in circles. What's left to talk about?"

"Us. What's going on. Where we go from here."

"We did that last night. We decided to remain *friends*—" God, that word sounded empty "—remember?"

"Yeah," he said with a glance at the car's hood, "that seems to be working real well."

"Well it would have if you hadn't come over," she snapped.

"Ah." Connor nodded slowly, his deep-blue eyes hazy with an emotion she couldn't quite read and wasn't sure she wanted to. "So the secret to us handling this is to stay the hell away from each other?"

"Apparently."

"And our friendship?"

Emma looked up at him and felt her defenses crumbling. If he stayed much longer, she just might do something totally idiotic, like throw herself into his arms and say to hell with doing the smart thing. But that wouldn't solve anything. It would only serve to make this harder eventually. Because she knew that Connor wasn't looking for love.

Heck, he never dated the same woman more than three times.

He wasn't a man to build fantasies around, even if she was still into daydreaming. Which she most certainly was *not.* She'd learned her lesson about love. And this time she'd take her lumps in private. Connor would never know that she was hurt. She wouldn't let him close enough to see that he had the power to crush her—whether he wanted it or not.

Tony Demarco's betrayal had hurt her.

When Connor did the same thing, it would kill her.

Nope.

She wouldn't let that happen.

"I'm not going to lose what we have," Connor said, when she didn't answer him. He stepped close enough to drop both hands onto her shoulders and squeeze. "Damn it, Emma, I *like* you. The *real* you. I like spending time with you and I don't want to lose that."

He *liked* her and she was in *love*. Oh, yeah. Fate had a twisted sense of humor.

"We've already lost it, Connor."

His hands tightened on her shoulders. "What's that supposed to mean?"

She swallowed hard, yanked free of his grip and turned her back on him, headed for the office. He caught up with her in a few long strides, grabbed her upper arm and turned her around to face him. His grip on her arm felt strong and warm. And the thought of never feeling his hands on her again made her want to whimper.

But because she was feeling just a little shaky, she straightened her spine, lifted her chin and met his gaze squarely. "You know just what it means. How are we supposed to pretend nothing's changed when everything has changed?"

"There's a way," he said.

"Well, when you find it, you let me know."

Connor's brain scrambled, trying to keep up with Emma. Wasn't easy, either. Not when his blood was still pumping and his body was still hot and eager.

But looking into her eyes now made Connor *want* to say the right thing. Somehow or other, he'd lost control of whatever it was between them. Not that he'd ever really had control.

Damn it, she'd been *engaged*. To some clown who'd hurt her. And now he was hurting her, too. The one thing he hadn't wanted to do, he'd ended up doing, just the same. Really pissed him off. And left him with a helpless feeling that he wasn't used to experiencing.

"I think you should just go, Connor."

Her voice, small and quiet, snapped him out of his thoughts and back to the moment.

Instinctively he reached for her again. She stepped back, avoiding his touch, and he felt the sting of it jab at him. His hand fisted on emptiness and dropped to his side. Something dark and cold settled in his gut, and Connor had the distinct impression that it was there to stay.

"Emma—"

"Just go. Please."

He blinked at her, too surprised to speak. Momentarily. "You're telling me to leave?"

She gave him a sad smile. "I'm *asking* you to leave."

He swallowed hard and battled a growing sense of desperation. In all the time they'd known each other, they'd never been so far apart. And even though she was just an arm's reach away, Connor had the feeling that with every passing second, she drifted even further from him.

She sighed and lifted one hand to rub at her forehead again. Guilt zapped him. Damn it, he hadn't meant to make her feel bad. Hadn't meant to start an argument that had no beginning and no end. Hadn't meant to *hurt* her.

Hadn't even meant to come here tonight.

Just like he didn't want to leave her now. Not when nothing had been settled. Not when she looked so damn...*sad*. But if he stayed, he'd only make this worse. She didn't want him here, fine.

He'd go.

For now.

Nodding, he choked back his own wants and said. "Okay, I'll go."

She gave him a smile that was so small, it was hardly worth the effort. But he appreciated it just the same.

"Thanks."

"This isn't over," he said before he stepped past her and opened the door. He stopped on the flower-bedecked porch and felt the warm summer air wrap itself around him. Looking back over his shoulder at her, he worked up a half-assed smile and said softly, "Please lock the door, Emma."

# Eleven

Emma buried herself in work.

For the past three days, she'd done tune-ups and oil changes and rebuilt two carburetors. She gave her mechanics a few days off and handled everything herself to make sure she kept busy. For three days she concentrated solely on the garage, and when she ran out of cars to work on, she replanted the flower beds.

Anything to keep from thinking about Connor.

And still it didn't help.

Mary Alice had sympathized and even offered to send her husband out to beat up Connor. But Emma didn't want him bruised—she wanted him to love her. Which wasn't going to happen.

Standing in the garage bay, she glanced toward where the car they'd made love on had been parked. And though the car was gone now, the memories remained.

Every touch, every sigh, every whisper was as fresh and clear in her mind as if it had just happened. She remembered his smile, the shine in his eyes and the feel of his hands on her skin. Her body ached for him and her heart just plain *ached.*

"Oh, man…" She set the torque wrench down and rubbed her eyes with the tips of her fingers. She hadn't slept more than a few hours in the past three days. Up at dawn, she worked late at the shop, trying to avoid sleep because every time she closed her eyes, Connor appeared in living color.

She'd done this to herself, she knew. She'd walked into this with her eyes wide-open—and her heart undefended. But she hadn't ever considered that it would be in danger. How could she have guessed that the love she used to dream about would be found in the arms of her best friend?

"And the worst part," she said, picking up the wrench again and squeezing it tightly, "is that I can't talk to my *best friend* about any of it. And darn it, Connor, I *miss* you."


The sun was bright, the sky clear and the ocean calm. In short, it was the perfect day for some saltwater fishing. A couple of times a season, Brian borrowed a little sport fisher boat from one of his pilot buddies, and the four Reilly brothers had a long day at sea—away from phones and work. Ordinarily Connor would have enjoyed the day out with his brothers.

Today he was forcing himself just to pay attention. Disgusted, Connor shifted his gaze from the frothing sea to the deck, where his brothers gathered around an open cooler.

"I'm telling you," Aidan said, pausing to take a sip of beer, "the wind was so high, the chopper was rocking back and forth like somebody was trying to shake us out. J.T. had hold of the stick with both hands, fighting to keep us steady. Right under us, the Sunday sailor's clinging to the upended bottom of his boat and he's holding on for dear life."

"Probably glad to see you then, huh?" Brian smiled and snapped his right wrist back, then forward, casting his line out into the ocean. Then he stuck the bottom of his rod into the pole holder on the side of the boat and set the bale on the reel. Leaning back, he watched Aidan and waited for the rest of the story.

"See that's the deal," Aidan went on, looking from one brother to the next with mock outrage. "There I am, jumping out of a chopper into storm surf—the waves were seven, maybe ten feet high—just to save this guy's ungrateful butt and does he thank me? Hell no, he takes a swing at me when I try to get him into the rescue basket."

"What?" Liam sounded incredulous, but Aidan's

story didn't surprise Connor. People always reacted weird in a panic situation. Which is why Marines came in so handy during a disaster. Cool heads.

And God knew Aidan needed a cool head doing his job. Working on the USMC sea rescue team, they were the guys called out to help stranded boaters or pick up pilots after they'd ditched their planes in the sea. The job was hard, dangerous and right up his brother's alley.

Aidan laughed. "No shit. The guy's panicked. Won't let go of the hull of his boat. Water's slapping at him, wind's howling, and he won't let go of the damn boat. Finally, he pries one hand off to take that swing at me, tells me he's afraid of heights and he wants us to send a ship out for him."

"A ship?" Liam asked laughing. "You mean like the one that sunk out from under him?"

"Exactly." Aidan leaned back against the side of the boat and drew both knees up, resting his forearms atop them.

"So how'd you get him in the basket?" Connor asked, drawn into the story in spite of the turmoil racing in his mind.

Aidan laughed. "I climbed into the basket myself and said, 'see ya.' The guy was so stunned that I'd leave him out there, he let go of the hull and jumped at the basket. I got out, got him in and Monk hoisted him up." He shook his head and sighed fondly. "Hell of a ride."

"Yeah, yeah, Mr. Hero," Brian teased and walked toward the hatch leading to the galley below deck.

"Come on, hero. Help me carry up that mountain of sandwiches Tina made for us."

"Tina made food?" Aidan asked, clearly worried. "Is it safe?"

"Hey," Brian complained as he started down the short flight of steps. "She's getting better."

Aidan groaned and muttered, "She couldn't get any worse without killing us."

"Yeah, well," Brian said, chuckling, "Tina's not real fond of you, so maybe you should watch what you eat."

"What d'you mean she's not fond of me?" Aidan's voice was outraged. "I'm the *fun* one!"

But he followed Brian out of the sunshine into the galley, leaving Liam and Connor alone on deck. The screech of the seagulls sounded weird and otherworldly in the silence. Off in the distance a sailboat caught the wind and flew across the ocean's surface, its red sails bellied, as it raced toward the horizon. Overhead, clouds scuttled across a deep-blue sky and briefly blotted out the sun's heat.

Connor sighed and focused his gaze on the distant spot where sky and sea met, blurring the lines of both. In the quiet, the gentle smack of the water against the hull was soothing, but didn't seem to help the thoughts churning in his mind.

He probably shouldn't have gone along with his brothers today. But if he'd tried to get out of it, he'd have had to come up with explanations he wasn't ready to make.

"Want to tell me what's going on?" Liam asked and sat perched on the edge of the boat's stern. He braced his hands on his knees and waited.

Connor flicked him a glance, then shifted his gaze back to the horizon's edge. "Nope."

Liam nodded, reached out and fiddled with the reel on Connor's fishing rod.

"What're you doing?"

"The bale was locked. Anything nibbles at your line, you lose the rod."

Connor sighed. Hell, he hadn't made that mistake since he was a kid and their father had taken them all out on the half-day fishing boats. "Thanks."

"You're welcome."

Liam fell into silence, gaze fixed on Connor until he shifted uneasily under that steady stare. "What're you looking at?"

"A man with a problem."

Major understatement, Connor thought, but kept his mouth shut. He just wasn't the kind of guy who needed to "vent" his feelings. He'd never wanted to hug and cry and learn and grow. He didn't mind listening to his friends' problems when they needed someone to talk to. But his own problems remained just that. His own.

"Knock it off, Liam."

"Hey, just sitting here."

"Well, sit somewhere else."

"It's a small boat," his brother said, shrugging.

"Getting smaller every damn minute," Connor

muttered. He lifted his right foot and braced it on the stern. "Don't you have a rosary to say or something?"

Liam grinned, unoffended. "I'm taking the day off."

"Lucky me."

"True."

"What?"

Liam smiled again. "You are lucky, Connor. You have a career you love, a family willing to put up with you and a beautiful day to do some fishing. So, you want to tell me why you look like a man who just lost his best friend?"

That last, stray statement hit a little close to home, and Connor winced. He stood up, walked to the edge of the boat and braced both hands on the gleaming wood railing. He shot Liam a quick look, then shifted his gaze back to the unending, rolling sea. "I think I *have* lost my best friend."

"Ahh…"

Connor snorted in disgust. "Don't give me Father Liam's patented, generic, sympathetic sigh."

"You want more specific sympathy, tell me what's going on."

"It's Emma."

"I figured that much out already." When Connor looked at him again, Liam shrugged. "Not that hard to work out, Connor. You lost the bet to her and now I'm thinking you lost something else to her as well."

"Like?"

"Your heart?"

Connor jerked up straight, as if he'd been shot. He

viciously rubbed the back of his neck, then pushed that hand into the pocket of his jeans shorts. "Nobody said anything about love."

"Until now," Liam mused.

"You know," Connor pointed out with a sidelong glare, "you can be pretty damn annoying for a brother, *Father.*"

"So I've heard." Liam stood up, too, and faced his younger brother. "Talk to me, Connor."

With a quick glance at the galley steps to make sure Brian and Aidan were still out of earshot, Connor blurted, "I think I'm losing my mind." Then he glared at his older brother. "And it's all your fault. The stupid bet. That's what started all this."

"Ahh…" Liam turned his face away to hide his smile. He wasn't entirely successful.

Connor muttered, "That's great. Laugh at your own brother's misery."

"What's a brother for?"

The boat rocked, sea spray drifted with the breeze and, overhead, seagulls kept watch, looking for supper.

"What's making you miserable?" Liam asked.

"Emma."

"This is getting better."

"Damn it, Liam." Connor stalked to the corner of the boat, then turned around and came back again. "Something's wrong."

Liam frowned. "With Emma? Is she okay?"

"*She's* okay. I'm the one in trouble."

"Oh."

Connor blew out a breath and viciously rubbed his face with both hands before dropping them to his sides. He couldn't believe this was happening. Not to him. Not to the man who'd firmly believed that the reason God had created so many beautiful women was to make love and marriage unnecessary.

All his life, one woman had been pretty much like the next. He'd figured if he lost one, there'd be another one right around the corner. Now? Now the only woman he wanted, didn't want *him*.

It had been three long days since the night he'd left Emma in her shop. Three days and three even-longer nights.

He'd tried everything he knew to keep his mind off her. He'd thought about asking some other woman out, but he just couldn't work up any interest in someone who wasn't Emma. He'd gone to his favorite hangout, but every time he saw that pool table, he saw Emma, stretched across it, her perfect legs tormenting him. Hell, he couldn't even work on his car without thinking about her.

His dreams were full of her image and every waking thought eventually wandered back to her. His chest felt tight every time he realized that she just might not want to see him again. Unconsciously he rubbed his chest with one hand and looked at Liam. "She won't talk to me."

"Does she have a reason?"

"Maybe." Remembering the look on her face when she'd told him about the idiot Tony, Connor winced. He hadn't been looking for a relationship. Hadn't wanted one. Hadn't expected to find one.

He'd lived his life pretty much on his own terms and had never considered changing. So *why*, he wanted to know, did the fact that Emma wouldn't talk to him, hurt him badly enough to make his whole insides ache with it?

Love?

Inwardly he reared back from the thought. Love? *Him?* Panic chewed on him.

He didn't *do* love.

"Hell," Connor muttered, still trying to get over the shock of what he might be feeling, "I really don't know anything anymore."

"Never thought I'd hear *you* say something like that."

"What?" Connor asked wryly, "a priest doesn't believe in miracles?"

"Good point." Liam leaned against the stern, crossed his arms over his chest and stared at him. "What are you going to do about this, Connor?"

He shook his head. "I think I've done enough already." Hell, he'd made his best friend throw him out of her place. He'd fixed it so she wouldn't talk to him. So she couldn't stand the sight of him. Oh, yeah. His work was done.

"So you're gonna quit? Walk away?"

Connor fixed him with an evil look. "You're manipulating me."

"No kidding."

"And who said anything about quitting?"

"Then, what's the plan?"

"If I knew that, would I be standing here being insulted by you?"

Liam grinned. "Okay, but aren't you the guy who said, and I think I'm quoting here, 'the day I need advice on women from a priest is the day they can shave my head and send me to Okinawa'?"

Man, the hits just kept on coming. Blowing out a breath, Connor grumbled, "Fine. I'm an idiot. I need advice."

Liam slapped one hand on his brother's shoulder. "Then here it is. You've already opened your eyes about Emma—maybe it's time you opened your heart."

"That's it?" he asked. "That's all you've got?"

Liam laughed. "Think about it, grasshopper. The answers will come."

"*Before* I'm old and gray?"

Probably." Liam bent and opened the cooler. "Want a beer?"


"Open my heart." Connor snorted and stepped out of his car into the humid night air. Liam's words echoed in his mind as they had all day. He looked at the garage, the light gleaming behind the windows and knew Emma was in there. His stomach fisted like he was about to tiptoe through a minefield.

Love?

Was he in love with Emma? He still didn't know the answer to that one.

He *liked* her. More than he ever had anyone else. It bothered hell out of him that they weren't speaking. That she didn't want to see him. And it really bothered hell out of him that he couldn't think about anything *but* Emma.

"But that's all going to change now," he murmured. It had taken him most of the day to figure out what Liam's advice had meant. Then it had finally hit him.

Stop treating Emma like his *friend* and start treating her like a *woman*.

He smiled to himself as he reached into the car and pulled out the white-tissue-paper-wrapped bouquet of red roses. Their scent was heavy, cloying and just right. Still smiling, he held the flowers in his left hand and grabbed up the gold foil box of expensive chocolates.

Finally. He felt in control.

This he knew.

"*This* I'm good at." Hell, he could write a how-to book for guys on how to smooth talk a woman out of being mad. Flowers, chocolate and a few kisses had bailed him out of trouble with women more times than he could count.

All he had to do was show her that he appreciated her. Show her that what they'd found was more than a one-night—or two-night—stand. Then, once she was softened up, they could find a way to deal with the changes in their relationship.

He straightened up, kicked the car door closed

and headed for the garage. Automatically he tried the doorknob and was pleased to find she'd locked it. "At least she listened about that."

Clutching the box of candy, he rapped the door with his knuckles and waited what felt like forever for her to answer. When she did, she opened the door only a few inches and peered out at him.

Through that narrow opening, he could see only one of her beautiful eyes and the tips of her fingers wrapped around the edge of the door. Partially hidden as if protecting herself, she was wearing the gray coveralls again, and a part of him wondered if she was naked beneath it. But then his body stirred and his mouth went dry, so he attempted to steer his brain away from the roller-coaster ride it was headed for.

"Connor. What're you doing here?"

"I needed to see you, Em," he said, and lifted the roses and candy, just in case she hadn't spotted them. "And I wanted to bring you these."

"Roses."

He smiled and took a step closer. "And candy."

She laughed shortly, a harsh, stiff sound that held no humor, and pushed the door a bit more closed. "You still don't get it."

Confused, he frowned and stared at her. "Get what? I'm just trying to be nice, here. What's going on, Emma?"

She looked at him for a long, silent minute. Connor could have sworn he could actually *hear* his own heartbeat in the deafening quiet. Then at last she opened the door wider and stepped out from behind it. Folding her arms across her chest, she shook her head and stared up at him.

Only then did he see the sheen of emotion glistening in her eyes. And he knew, instinctively, that he'd done something wrong. But for the life of him, he couldn't figure out *what*.

"You brought me roses."

"So?"

"I hate roses."

Something clicked in the back of his brain and he wanted to kick himself. He'd *known* that, damn it. Known that Emma's favorite flowers were carnations. His left hand squeezed the bouquet tightly as if he were hoping he could just make the damn flowers disappear. But he couldn't, so he said, "You're right. I didn't think. I—"

Emma lifted her chin and stared into his eyes. To Connor's horror, those beautiful eyes of hers filled with tears, and he prayed like hell they wouldn't spill over.

"No, you didn't think," she said sadly. "Not about *me*. You bought me your traditional make-up present and figured that would do it."

"Emma…" This wasn't going the way he'd planned. Nothing was working out. He was getting in deeper and felt the quicksand beneath his feet sucking at him.

Desperation clawed at him as he realized that by trying to make things better between them, he'd only made them worse.

"I told you three days ago, Connor," she said, her voice still just a low, disappointed hush, "the foo-foo girl thing is *not* me. The me you were with before doesn't exist. Not really. And the me I really am, you don't want."

His insides trembled, and he scrambled to find the right words to say. But nothing was coming to him. The one time he needed the ability to smooth talk, he was coming up empty.

He'd hurt her again.

And that knowledge delivered a pain to his soul like nothing he'd ever known before.

Suddenly it was more important than it had been to get through to her. He felt as though he was sliding down a rocky cliff, trying to grab something to stop his fall. But there was nothing there. "Emma, I know I did this wrong..." He let his hands, still holding the offerings she hadn't wanted, fall to his sides. "I just wanted us to be friends again."

"I don't want to be your *friend*, Connor."

Her voice was too small, too hushed, too full of pain, and every word she spoke fell like a rock into the bottom of his heart. "Why the hell not?"

"Because I love you, Connor."

"Emma—"

"Don't say anything, okay?" She held one hand up for quiet. "Please." She choked out a laugh that sounded as though it had scraped her throat. "This is my fault and I'll get over it—*trust me*." She inhaled sharply, deeply, then blew it all out again, lifting one hand to swipe at a single, stray tear glistening on her cheek.

Connor's chest tightened as though he were in a giant vise and some unseen hand was forcing it closed around him. He couldn't breathe. His heart hurt, his hands ached to hold her and he *knew*, without a doubt, that if he tried to reach for her, Emma would turn him away. And he didn't know if he could take that.

So instead he stood there like an idiot while the woman who meant so much to him battled silent tears.

"I can't be your lover anymore, Connor," she said and he swallowed hard at the calm steadiness in her eyes. "It would kill me to have you and yet never have you—you know? And I can't be your friend anymore, either—"

She gulped in air and kept talking, her words rushing from her in a flood of emotion that was thick enough to choke both of them.

"Emma—"

"No. I can't be your buddy and listen to you complain about the women in your life. I don't want to hear about the date of the week or the hot brunette who caught your eye."

Guilt raged inside him and battled with another, stronger feeling that was suddenly so real, so desperate, he trembled with the force of it.

For the first time in his life, Connor felt helpless.

And he didn't like it one damn bit.

"Go away, Connor," she said as another tear slid

down her cheek. Stepping back from the doorway, she pushed the door closed. As she did, she said softly, "And do us both a favor, okay? This time when you go? Stay away."

Then the door closed, and Connor, the damn roses in one hand and a box of chocolates in the other, was left standing alone in the growing darkness.

Despite the hot summer night, he felt cold to the bone.

# Twelve

The next morning Emma had a pickup truck that needed a new timing belt, an SUV with bad brakes and a headache that wouldn't quit.

Too many tears and not enough sleep.

And the way she was feeling, she didn't see things changing anytime soon.

For most of the night she'd agonized over blurting out her love to Connor. *Why* hadn't she just kept her big mouth shut? Bracing her elbows on her desktop, she cupped her face in her hands and tried desperately to forget the look on his face when she'd said the three little words designed to inspire panic in the hearts of men everywhere.

"Oh, God." She swallowed hard and took a deep

breath. "Emma, you idiot. You never should have said it. Now he *knows*. Now he's probably feeling *sorry* for you. Oh, man…"

She jumped up from the desk, started for the door to the garage bay, then changed her mind and whipped around, walking toward the bank of windows instead. She couldn't go into the garage. She didn't want to talk to the guys. Didn't want them wondering why her eyes were all red. Didn't want anyone else knowing that she'd allowed her heart to be flattened by an emotional sledgehammer.

"Maybe I could sell the shop," she whispered. "Leave town—no, leave the state." Then she caught herself and muttered, "Great. Panic. Good move."

She wasn't going to leave. Wasn't going to hide.

What she *was* going to do, was live her life. Pretend everything was normal and good until eventually, it *would* be. Positive mental attitude. That was the key. She'd just keep her thoughts positive and her tears private.

Everything would work out.

Everything would be good again.

"God, I'm such a liar." Sighing, Emma thought about going home, but that wouldn't solve anything. At least here, in the shop, she had things to concentrate on. She could catch up on paperwork.

Of course, what she wanted to do was lie down somewhere in the dark and go to sleep. Then hopefully, when she woke up again, her heart would be healed and she'd be able to think of Connor without wanting to either hug him or slug him.

But it wouldn't be that easy, she knew.

She was going to have to deal with Connor—at least until he was transferred to another base or deployed overseas or something. She'd have to find a way to learn to live with what had happened between them. Learn to survive with her heart breaking.

Shouldn't take her more than ten or twenty years. "Piece of cake."

A florist's van pulled into the driveway off Main Street and Emma nearly groaned. Oh, God, more flowers. Last night he'd brought the "Gee, I'm sorry, please forgive me" bouquet. What was up today? she wondered. Maybe a little something from the "Too bad you're in love and I'm not" sympathy line?

"This just keeps getting more and more humiliating," she said as she hit the front door and marched across the parking lot to head off the delivery guy.

The sun was hot, the air was stifling, and even the asphalt beneath her feet felt as if it was on fire. All around her, Baywater was going about its business. Behind her in the garage bay, she heard the whir of the air compressor. Kids played, moms shopped, guys cruised in their cool cars, looking for a girl to spend some time with.

And here, in this one little corner of town, Emma

prepared to take a stand. She didn't want Connor's pity bouquets. She didn't want his guilt.

All she wanted now was to speed up time so that this whole mess could be safely in her past.

"Emma Jacobsen?" The delivery driver shouted as he jumped down from the van, holding a long, white box, tied with a bright purple ribbon.

"Yes," she said, remembering that the flowers weren't *this* guy's fault. He was just doing his job. "But if those are for me, you can just take them right back."

"Huh?" He was just a kid. Couldn't have been more than eighteen. His almost-white blond hair stood up in spikes at the top of his head, and he pulled his sunglasses down to peer at her over the rim. "You don't *want* 'em?"

"No, I don't." Be strong, she told herself. Be firm. Be *positive*.

He laughed and shoved his glasses back up his nose. "He *said* you'd say that, but I didn't believe him. I never had anybody say no before."

"Happy to be your first," she snarled, really annoyed that Connor had *predicted* that she wouldn't want his latest attempt at reconciliation. Turning sharply, she headed back for the shop, but the kid's voice stopped her.

"Hey, wait a minute. He told me to tell you something if you said no."

She shouldn't care.

But damn it, she *did*.

"Fine." Emma squared her shoulders and turned back to glare at him. "What?"

"Sheesh, lady, don't shoot the messenger."

"Sorry." She inhaled sharply, then let the air slide from her lungs in an attempt to cool down. "What?"

"The guy said to say—" he screwed up his face trying to remember every word "—are you too chicken to even look?"

"Chicken?" she repeated, amazed. "He actually said *chicken?* What? Is he in fifth grade or something?" She frowned at the kid. "You're sure he said 'chicken'?"

"Yeah." The kid shrugged, still holding the long white box crooked easily in one arm. "So. Are you? Chicken, I mean? No offense."

"None taken," she said, then stomped toward him. "Fine. I'll take them." Even though she *knew* Connor was manipulating her into it. He'd known darn well that she'd respond to a dare. Her heart twisted a bit. How could he know her so well *and* so little?

"Sign here."

She did, then took the box, which was a lot heavier than she expected it to be. She shot the kid a quizzical look.

He shrugged. "You got me, lady. I just deliver 'em." Then with a wave he jumped back into the van and pulled out of the lot.

Emma carried the box back to the office and set it on top of the desk. Her fingers danced across the lid, as she decided whether or not to open it. The ribbon felt cool and slick and the gold seal beneath the ribbon read Scentsabilities, the exclusive flower and gift shop at the outskirts of town.

"Fine," she muttered, glaring at the box as if it were a personal challenge—which, she admitted, it *was.* "I'll look. That doesn't mean I'll *keep.*"

She pulled the ribbon off, lifted the lid and then poked through several layers of pale-blue and green tissue paper. She stopped and stared. Her breath caught. Hot tears filled her eyes, and her lower lip trembled as she smiled and reached into the box.

A single white carnation lay atop a collection of brand-new, top-of-the-line, *socket wrenches.*

"Oh, Connor," she said, running her fingertips over the cool, stainless-steel tools. "You wonderful nut."

He'd touched her, damn it. He'd known just how to do it and he'd touched her heart again. Why? Why was he doing it? What did it mean? And how could she keep her heart from jumping to dangerous conclusions?

"What're you doing, Connor? And why're you doing it?" She dropped into her desk chair, holding the single carnation close to her heart—and tried desperately not to read too much into this.

Connor had a plan.

He'd spent most of the night coming up with it, and now all he had to do was wait and see if it would work.

Leaving Emma the night before had been the hardest thing he'd ever done. Forget boot camp. Forget active duty in a war zone. They were nothing.

Walking away from a woman you'd hurt was immeasurably worse. Especially when that woman meant more to you than you'd ever realized. Why is it that you never really knew how important someone was until you'd lost them?

He'd been up all night, figuring out what to do, figuring out just what he *wanted* to do.

At first, he hadn't been able to think beyond the memory of Emma's tear-stained face and heartbroken voice. He'd stalled and relived that moment over and over again before it had dawned on him what the answer was to the situation.

And once he'd faced the truth, the solution was blindingly simple.

The answer was *Emma*.

Always *Emma*.

He couldn't imagine his life without her in it.

For two years they'd laughed together and worked together and talked about anything and everything. She'd been the center of most of his days, and he'd never picked up on it. Then finally, because of that stupid bet... The nights he'd spent with her in his arms were the most perfect he'd ever experienced. He'd found magic with Emma. A magic that had slipped up on him. Magic he'd almost lost through his own stupidity.

Now all he had to do was convince Emma that he was smart enough to recognize the best thing that had ever happened to him.

Bright and early the next morning, Emma stumbled into the dimly lit kitchen, looking for coffee. She pushed her hair out of her eyes and tossed a glance at the still-silent phone.

She'd expected Connor to call her last night.

Naturally, he hadn't.

"The man never does what you expect," she murmured and grabbed a blue ceramic coffee cup out of the cupboard and turned for the coffeepot. She poured herself a cupful, then headed to the back porch to drink it.

She stepped into the early-morning cool and sighed as a soft breeze caressed her bare legs. Soon enough, the summer heat would start simmering Baywater in its own juices. But now, in the minutes before dawn, the air was fresh and sweet and still-damp with dew.

Swinging her long hair back over her shoulders, she sat down on the top step and cradled her cup between her palms. The rich coffee scent stirred her mind and opened her eyes. She took a sip and felt the liquid caffeine hit her system like a blessing.

Thoughts of Connor had again kept her up most of the night, but this time there'd been fewer tears and more questions. The socket wrenches had been a balm to her bruised heart. He'd seen *her*. Paid attention to *her*.

"That's something, isn't it?" she wondered aloud.

"Talking to yourself's a bad sign."

She sucked in a breath and whipped her head around. "Connor? What're you doing here?"

"Wishing I had some of that coffee, for starters," he said, and walked through the garden gate off the driveway. He wore jeans and a dark-blue T-shirt that hugged every rippling muscle of his chest.

She watched him come closer and wished to high heaven she'd taken the time to at least brush her hair. Or get dressed. Good God, she was wearing her summer pj's—a pair of men's boxers and a dark-pink tank top with a teddy bear on the front. Curling up smaller on the step, she flashed Connor a frown. "You shouldn't be here."

"I had to be here," he said and reached out to grab her coffee cup. Taking a sip, he sighed, then smiled and handed it back. "You look beautiful."

"Oh, yeah. Right."

"I'm the one doing the looking, aren't I?"

His gaze drifted over her in a lazy perusal, and Emma felt her blood begin to boil. Her skin felt hot and tingly. Her breath was strangled in her throat, and her heart pounded like a bass drum in a Fourth of July parade.

She scooped her hair back from her face and blew out a fast breath. "Why are you here?"

"To show you something."

"More wrenches?"

He grinned and her heart sped up. "You liked 'em?"

"Yes," she said, lips twitching. "Thank you."

"You're welcome." He held out one hand toward her. "Now, come with me."

"Connor…" She lifted her gaze from his outstretched hand to his eyes. "You don't have to—"

He grabbed her hand and pulled her to her feet with such strength she flew at him, her chest slamming into his. He wrapped one arm around her waist, looked down into her eyes and said, "Just trust me, Em. This one time, will you just trust me?"

Emma would have agreed to anything while his body was pressed to hers. She felt his heartbeat thundering in time with hers, and shockwaves of sensation rocketed through her. Despite how good it felt to be close to him again though, Emma had to at least attempt to protect herself. Pulling back, she looked up at him and nodded. "Okay. Five minutes. Then I'm going inside and you're going home."

He smiled and lifted one hand, running the tips of his fingers along her jawline. "Five minutes, then."

He tightened his grip on her hand and dragged her behind him as he stalked across the yard toward the gate. A wooden lattice arch rose over the garden gate, and deep-blue morning glories spread their beauty and scent along the rungs. He drew her under the arch and through the gate, saying, "Close your eyes."

"Connor…"

"Five minutes, Em."

"Fine." She closed her eyes and stumbled barefoot

behind him. The dewy grass became river stone pavers and then the already-warming asphalt of the driveway. Emma held on to Connor's hand, and in a corner of her mind she told herself to enjoy this. The feel of his hand on hers. The joy of seeing him first thing in the morning. The sparkle in his eyes and the warmth of his smile.

Then he came to a stop and announced, "Open your eyes, Emma."

She did and immediately gasped aloud. Dropping her hold on his hand, she walked toward the banged-up, rusted, completely ruined hulk of a '58 Corvette. Its red paint had oxidized, the chrome bumpers were peeling and crumpled, the leather seats were cracked and springing out in tufts of cotton batting.

And it was the most beautiful thing she'd ever seen.

Whirling around to face him, she said, "How? How did you get Mrs. Harrison to part with Sonny's car?"

"You like it?"

"*Duh*." She glanced over her shoulder at the car, as if to make sure it hadn't disappeared in the last moment or two. "But how? And how'd you get it here?"

He shoved his hands into his jeans pockets. "I went to see her yesterday," he said. "I convinced her that Sonny's car deserved to be everything it was *meant* to be."

"You did?"

"Yep." He smiled proudly and she couldn't blame him for it. "As to getting it here, Aidan has a friend with a tow truck. We unhooked it at the end of your street and pushed it up your driveway so we wouldn't wake you up." He rolled his eyes. "Surprised you didn't wake up, anyway, with all of Aidan's whining about it. Almost gagged him."

"I can't believe you did this," she whispered, looking from him, to the car and back again.

He shrugged and added, "I also promised Mrs. Harrison that once we'd restored the 'Vette to its former glory, that we'd come out and take her for the first ride."

*"We?"*

"Caught that, did you?" he smiled, and took a step toward her.

She took a deep, steadying breath. "Connor, no one's ever done anything like this for me before. I don't even know what to say."

"Good," he said quickly, stepping forward and grabbing her shoulders. "Speechless. That means I've got a shot to have my say."

"Now just a darn—"

"Too late," he said, talking over her, his drill sergeant's voice drowning her out with no problem at all. "My turn, Em." He slid his right hand from her shoulder to her neck and up, to cup her cheek. "I see *you,* Emma. The *real* you."

His thumb traced her cheekbone with long, gentle strokes, and he silently prayed that for once in his life, he'd find the right words. The words he needed to win this woman—because without her his life looked long and lonely.

"Last night, when you closed the door and sent me away," he said, shaking his head slowly, as if unable to bear the remembered pain of being shut out, "I finally *knew.*"

"What?"

"I love you, Emma Jacobsen."

"Oh, Connor," she whispered, "no, you don't."

"Yeah. I do."

His voice was steely and every word stood on its own, loud and proud. Her eyes went wide and filled with tears, but she blinked them away, for which he was grateful.

"Hey, surprised me, too," he said, a strained, half laugh choking him. "I'd always thought that I didn't need love. That my life was fine, just the way it was. But the only reason it *was* fine, is because *you* were in it." He cupped her face between his palms and stared directly into her eyes. "When something good happens, *you're* the one I want to share it with. When I feel like hell and nothing's going right, I head right here—to talk to *you.*"

She reached up and covered his hands with hers. "Connor, I…"

"Without you, Em, there's no laughter." He shook his head and smiled down at her. "There's no warmth. There's only emptiness. And I don't want to live like that. I want to live with *you.* I want to marry you. Have babies with you. Build a *future* with you."

"You what?" She dropped her coffee cup, and it landed with a solid crash on the asphalt, spilling hot coffee as it went.

Instantly Connor scooped her into his arms and held her cradled close to his chest. "You okay?" he asked. "Burned? Cut?"

"I'm fine," she said on a whisper, lifting one hand to stroke his face. "Unless of course, I'm dreaming, in which case I'm really going to be disappointed when I wake up."

He smiled down at her, then bent his head and stole a quick kiss. "Not dreaming. In fact, I feel like I'm just waking up."

"I do love you," she said softly.

"I love you, too, Em," Connor said, smile gone and gaze steady on hers. "I want us to be like that old car. I want us to be what we *deserve* to be. Together."

Her heart felt full enough to explode, and her eyes blurred with tears of happiness so thick she could hardly see. And yet there he was, in all his blurry glory. He'd been her friend, then her lover and now, finally and forever, he would be her husband.

Emma blinked away her tears, because she wanted this moment to be clear in her memory. "I'll marry you, Connor. I'll have a family with you. And I promise I will love you forever."

"That's all I'll ever ask, Em," he said, and carried her beneath the arch of morning glories into the shade-dappled yard.

"That's all?" she teased.

"Well," he hedged, "that and a cup of coffee. I've been up all night, waiting for you to wake up."

"Then let's forget about the coffee," she said, reaching up to hook her arms around his neck, "and head right to bed."

Connor grinned. "You know, I think I'm gonna like being married."

Emma laughed aloud and hung on for dear life as she and her best friend started their new life together in the first sweet hush of dawn.

\* \* \* \* \*

*Maureen Child's*
**THREE WAY WAGER**
*series concludes next month in*
*Silhouette Desire.*
*Don't miss*
**THE LAST REILLY STANDING**
*available in July.*

# eHARLEQUIN.com

## The Ultimate Destination for Women's Fiction

### Visit eHarlequin.com's Bookstore today for today's most popular books at great prices.

- An extensive selection of romance books by top authors!

- Choose our convenient "bill me" option. No credit card required.

- New releases, Themed Collections and hard-to-find backlist.

- A sneak peek at upcoming books.

- Check out book excerpts, book summaries and Reader Recommendations from other members and post your own too.

- Find out what everybody's reading in Bestsellers.

- Save BIG with everyday discounts and exclusive online offers!

- Our Category Legend will help you select reading that's exactly right for you!

- Visit our Bargain Outlet often for huge savings and special offers!

- Sweepstakes offers. Enter for your chance to win special prizes, autographed books and more.

### Your purchases are 100% guaranteed—so shop online at www.eHarlequin.com today!

**Silhouette®**

**Desire.**

## Welcome to Silhouette Desire's brand-new installment of

*The drama unfolds for six of the state's wealthiest bachelors.*

## BLACK-TIE SEDUCTION
### by Cindy Gerard
(Silhouette Desire #1665, July 2005)

## LESS-THAN-INNOCENT INVITATION
### by Shirley Rogers
(Silhouette Desire #1671, August 2005)

## STRICTLY CONFIDENTIAL ATTRACTION
### by Brenda Jackson
(Silhouette Desire #1677, September 2005)

*Look for three more titles from Michelle Celmer, Sara Orwig and Kristi Gold to follow.*

# COMING NEXT MONTH

### #1663 BETRAYED BIRTHRIGHT—Sheri WhiteFeather
*Dynasties: The Ashtons*
When Walker Ashton decided to search for his past, he found it on a
Sioux Nation reservation. Helping him to deal with his Native American
heritage was Tamra Winter Hawk, a woman who cherished her roots
and had Walker longing for a future together. But when his real-world
commitments intruded upon their fantasy liaison, would they find a way
to keep the connection they'd formed?

### #1664 THE LAST REILLY STANDING—Maureen Child
*Three-Way Wager*
Aidan Reilly was determined to win the bet he'd made with his brothers.
Three months without sex meant one thing: spend *a lot* of time with his
best gal pal, Terry Evans. She had given up on love long ago because the
pain just wasn't worth it. Then…temptation proved to be too much. The last
Reilly standing had lost the bet, but could he win the girl?

### #1665 BLACK-TIE SEDUCTION—Cindy Gerard
*Texas Cattleman's Club: The Secret Diary*
Millionaire Jacob Thorne got on Christine Travers's last nerve—the sensible
lady had no time for Jacob's flirtatious demeanor. But when the two butted
heads at an auction, Jacob embarked on a black-tie seduction that would
prove she had needs—womanly needs—that only he could satisfy.

### #1666 THE RUGGED LONER—Bronwyn Jameson
*Princes of the Outback*
Australian widower Tomas Carlisle was stunned to learn he had to father
a child to inherit a cattle empire. Making a deal with longtime friend
Angelina Mori seemed the perfect solution—until their passion escalated
and Angelina mounted an all-out attack on Tomas's defense against hot,
passionate, *committed* love.

### #1667 CRAVING BEAUTY—Nalini Singh
They'd married within mere days of meeting. Successful tycoon
Marc Bordeaux had been enchanted by Hira Dazirah's desert beauty. But
Hira feared Marc only craved her outer good looks. This forced Marc to
prove his true feelings to his virgin bride—and tender actions spoke louder
than words.…

### #1668 LIKE LIGHTNING—Charlene Sands
Although veterinarian Maddie Brooks convinced rancher Trey Walker to
allow her to live and work on his ranch, there was no way Trey would ever
romance the sweet and sexy Maddie. He was a victim of the "Walker Curse"
and couldn't commit to any woman. But once they gave in to temptation,
Maddie was determined to make their arrangement more permanent.…